Good Enough

Good Enough

Paula Yoo

HARPER TEEN
An Imprint of HarperCollins Publishers

HarperTeen is an imprint of HarperCollins Publishers.

Good Enough
Copyright © 2008 by Paula Yoo
Library of Congress Cataloging-in-Publication Data
Yoo, Paula.
    Good enough / Paula Yoo. — 1st ed.
        p.   cm.
    Summary: A Korean American teenager tries to please her par-
ents by getting into an Ivy League school, but a new guy in school
and her love of the violin tempt her in new directions.
    ISBN 978-0-06-079085-1 (trade bdg.)
    ISBN 978-0-06-079089-9 (lib. bdg.)
    1. Korean Americans—Juvenile fiction. [1. Korean Americans—
Fiction. 2. Gifted children—Fiction. 3. Musicians—Fiction.
4. Violin—Fiction. 5. Parent and child—Fiction. 6. Self-
realization—Fiction.] I. Title.
PZ7.Y8156Go 2008   2007002985
[Fic]—dc22   CIP
                                                             AC

Typography by Sasha Illingworth
1 2 3 4 5 6 7 8 9 10
❖
First Edition

For my parents, Young and Kim Yoo,
who always believed I was more than good enough

Special thanks to . . .

Steve Malk, my agent,
for making my dream come true

Anne Hoppe, my editor,
for her brilliant editing insight and wisdom

David Yoo, my brother,
for his kindness and writing advice

Kyle McCorkle, my husband,
for everything

All my friends and family for their advice, support,
and encouragement during the writing of this novel

This book was made possible, in part,
by the Judy Blume Grant administered by the
Society of Children's Book Writers & Illustrators.

Good Enough

Pink Elephants

You've heard the joke, right? *Why is a viola better than a violin?* It burns longer.

Wait, here's another. *You're lost in the woods and meet a pink elephant and a good viola player. Who do you ask for directions?* The pink elephant—a good viola player is just a figment of your imagination.

Violists hate it when we violinists crack viola jokes. But my audition for the Connecticut All-State High School Orchestra is in ten minutes, and I'm trying to relax. I raise my bow above the strings, about to practice one last time. And that's when I hear it. This note.

This pure note, with a warm vibrato that could melt ice instantly, flows from a nearby trumpet. It floats across the room. My concentration's broken. That's never happened to me before.

I whirl around, looking for the source of the sound. Which isn't easy, because there are at least fifty trumpet players scattered throughout the lobby, practicing the same fanfare passage from Rimsky-Korsakov's *Capriccio Espagnol*, op. 34—one of the pieces the All-State Orchestra will perform at the annual concert next April.

It's eleven A.M. on the last Saturday of August, and auditions are being held at the University of Hartford's Hartt School, which is also where I have my violin lessons. Every year, students from all over Connecticut try out for a spot in the All-State Orchestra. Only the best are chosen, because we have to be technically advanced enough to practice the music to perfection on our own between now and April. Then we have an all-day rehearsal followed by a concert that evening. Students pack the lobby and nearby hallways, practicing furiously before their audition times. You've got a flautist doing C major arpeggios next to a cellist playing the first movement of the Boccherini Cello Concerto. And across from the cellist sits my friend Susan Summers, bobbing her head up and down as she runs through a difficult passage from a Vivaldi bassoon concerto. (I could insert a bassoon joke here,[1] but I like Susan, and she's a really good musician, even though, well, she plays the bassoon.)

I glance at my sheet music—for the solo part of my audition, I will play the first movement of Mendelssohn's Violin Concerto in E minor. I've won the first chair of All-State Concertmaster three years in a row. Being chosen concertmaster means you're the best violinist in the entire state. I'm hoping to win it again for my senior year. Getting concertmaster for the fourth straight year will look good on my college applications. Plus I know the Mendelssohn like the back of my hand. But the sixteenth notes splayed across the paper blur into a hazy, inky mess because I can't pay attention. Normally I can zone out all this white noise. What's wrong with me?

I duck as a neighboring violinist's bow nearly impales

[1] Q: Why did the chicken cross the road?
A: To get away from the bassoon recital.

my left ear. She ignores me and keeps practicing . . .the Mendelssohn. I pause and listen as she scrambles to hit all the notes—she rushes the beat and her intonation is sharp. I sigh, relieved she's not as good as me.

And then I spot him. The one who's distracting me from preparing for my audition. He's standing in the far left corner of the lobby. The blinking fluorescent lights sparkle off the bell of his trumpet. His eyes are closed, and he stands perfectly straight at attention, his left hand curled in a C shape around the valves of the trumpet. He's tall and lean, dressed neatly in a pair of faded jeans and a white Oxford shirt, the sleeves rolled up to the elbows. His wavy brown hair curls behind his ears, and long bangs cover his eyes.

For a moment I'm in another world, transfixed by each beautiful note that peals effortlessly from his lips. I'm glad he doesn't play violin, because then we'd have to compete against each other.

He finishes the fanfare. He lowers his trumpet and glances in my direction. He pushes a lock of hair away, and I notice how green his eyes are.

Silence. He's still staring at me. Too late, I realize he's caught me just standing here, gawking at him, my mouth partially open. My thick black-framed Harry Potter–style glasses slip down my nose. I push them up, wishing for the thousandth time that my nose wasn't so flat and that I didn't have the kind of pudgy Korean face that looks cute at age seven but not at age seventeen, and that I wasn't so short. Guys normally don't smile at me unless they're making fun of me for taking stuff like *Star Wars* a little too seriously or asking me to help tutor them in math. I look away from him, and I wonder why my heart is suddenly beating so fast.

While I'm thinking these thoughts, the cute trumpet guy walks right over, cradling the trumpet underneath his arm. He towers over me—I have to step back and crane my neck to see his eyes.

"Hi," he says.

All that floats through my brain is a trumpet joke. *How many trumpet players does it take to change a light bulb? Just one, but he'll do it too loudly.* (Oh my God. Stop it.)

Cute Trumpet Guy just stands there, waiting for me to say something. I'm tongue-tied because I'm mesmerized by his eyes, which are the exact same shade of green as that of pimento-stuffed olives. I don't even like olives.

"What's wrong?" he asks. Suddenly I realize I've been frowning this whole time.

"You're too loud." I wince. I can't believe I just said that. But it *is* true—he was too loud and I couldn't concentrate.

"Sorry," he says. But he doesn't sound upset. "Are you nervous about your audition?"

What? Excuse me? Did Cute Trumpet Guy just ask if the Three-Times-in-a-Row-All-State-Concertmaster was nervous?

"You have to try and zone everyone out," he continues. "It's hard, but you can do it."

I don't need his advice, but he sounds so sincere and nice that I can't help but smile. It's like he actually cares about me even though we don't know each other.

"What's your name?" he asks.

Before I can reply, someone shouts. "Patti Yoon?" A woman holding a clipboard scans the lobby. "Is Patti here?"

"I'm Patti Yoon," I say.

"Good. You're next."

I glance at the clock on the wall. It's 11:04 A.M. My audition is at 11:10 A.M. "But I don't play until—"

"We're running ahead of schedule, which is a first," the woman says. "Come on, Patti Yoon, we don't want to hold everyone up."

I didn't get to do my final run-through before the audition because of Cute Trumpet Guy. Now I've got to wing it with no net. Great. I head for the door.

"Hey."

I turn around. Cute Trumpet Guy follows me. He holds up my audition music. "You forgot this." You know, he has flecks of blue in those green-olive eyes.

He hands over my music. His fingers brush against mine as I take the music from him, the tissue-thin paper crackling in my hands. I can still feel the imprint of his fingers, warm against my skin, as he lets go.

"Thanks," I whisper.

And then he smiles. It's a lopsided smile, and he kind of tilts his head at the same time. A lock of wavy brown hair falls over his eyes.

Suddenly all the chaos in the lobby silences, and everyone disappears, and we are the only ones in the room. There's this weird rushing sound in my ears, as if I'm falling in slow motion off a cliff. When Cute Trumpet Guy speaks, he sounds so far away. "Good luck . . . Patti Yoon."

I suddenly wonder if pink elephants do exist.

Top Ten Reasons Why You Have a Bad Audition

1. Your hands, for some reason, won't stop shaking.
2. Who is Cute Trumpet Guy? What school does he go to? Why doesn't he cut his hair so it doesn't fall over his green-olive eyes? All this thinking distracts you, and you make a mistake during the easiest part of the piece.
3. An audition judge sighs and scribbles something down on a piece of paper. You lose your place in the music and have to start over.
4. Mendelssohn is hard.
5. Cute Trumpet Guy smiled at you! You lose count of the eighth-note passages and stumble. (The judge, meanwhile, sighs some more and keeps scribbling.)
6. Why didn't you wish Cute Trumpet Guy good luck before his audition? You're so upset by this oversight that you play a G natural instead of a G sharp. The judge winces.

7. Mendelssohn is really, really hard.
8. For some reason you start thinking about pimento olives. And then you keep playing a G natural instead of a G sharp. (The judge, scribbling, sighing, etc.)
9. You realize you don't know Cute Trumpet Guy's real name. This bugs you, and as a result, you end the piece on the wrong note.
10. You wonder if you will ever see Cute Trumpet Guy again.

How to Make Your Korean Parents Happy, Part 1

Get a perfect score on the SATs.

The 2300 Club

"At least I got a seven hundred in critical reading."

As if blowing my All-State audition last week wasn't bad enough, my SAT scores from the June test were just announced online this morning. All I had to do was go to the website, enter my password, and voilà! 700 Critical Reading, 620 Math, 690 Writing.

Silence. All I hear is the constant chopping sounds of my mom's kitchen knife against the wooden cutting board. *Chop chop chop.* She's chopping the cabbage while I clean the last of the mung beans, inspecting every single one and yanking off the nasty black part at the tip of each sprout. We're sitting at the kitchen table on a Saturday morning, making the weekly *mandoo* for tomorrow's church services while my dad is outside, mowing the lawn. The engine roars past the kitchen window, making it hard to hear, so my mom and I have been yelling at each other all morning in order to be heard. Which saves time, because sooner or later in our conversation we'll end up yelling anyway.

"But what about the six-twenty in math and the six-ninety in the writing section?" my mom asks.

"I'm sorry," I say, feeling miserable. I was sure I would score at least a 700 on each test. But *620*? In math? I cringe, reliving that moment just an hour ago when the scores popped up on my computer screen.

Chop chop chop. "That makes twenty ten," my mom says. Silence.

She doesn't have to say anything after that. I know what we're both thinking: THESE SAT SCORES ARE NOT GOOD ENOUGH. In other words, I'm not a member of the hallowed 2300 Club, that elite group of students who hit at least a 2300 or higher (2400 being the perfect score) on the SATs.

Technically speaking, there's nothing wrong with a 2010. Unless you are applying for HYP—Harvard,

Yale, Princeton. Or as my parents always say in this breathless yelp: *"HARVARDYALEPRINCETON."* I'm being groomed for the Ivy Leagues. Plus my parents are Korean. Which means that their American Dream is for Their Oldest Child to Be Accepted at Every Single Ivy League University in the Country So They Can Brag About It to Their Korean Friends.

It started when I was four years old. My parents had decided I should take up an instrument because I was the most physically uncoordinated student in preschool. (Scariest two words in the English language: *obstacle course.*) Shining in athletics was not an option for the future main extracurricular activity that would set me apart from other Ivy applicants.

See, straight As and getting a super high score on the SATs isn't good enough. You need a "hook" for the Ivy League. So thirteen years ago I was given a choice—the violin or the piano. I remember standing in the middle of the musical instrument store, next to a shiny black Baldwin grand piano. Above me dangled dozens of violins. I remember looking up and being mesmerized by the light pouring in from the store window, flickering across the varnished flame-striped maple surfaces of the violins. The store owner handed me a one-eighth-size violin and I plucked a string, marveling at the way the sound resonated through the wood and into my heart. Even though it was the first time I had held a violin, my left hand curled naturally around its neck, as if I had been born to play this instrument.

To my parents' relief, I turned out to be good at the violin. Actually I was more than good. I was *really* good. I was pretty much a B-tier violin prodigy. An A-tier prodigy is Sarah Chang, who ends up playing Paganini's Violin Concerto no. 1 with the New York Philharmonic by age eight and gets her picture in *The New York Times*. Then you've got your B-tier prodigy, like me, where technically I'm not a prodigy but I'm pretty close. The difference? I too will perform a violin concerto—the Mendelssohn—later this fall, but it will be with my youth orchestra and not the New York Phil, and my picture will end up in the *Hartford Courant* local neighborhood section instead of the front page of *The New York Times*. So why don't I apply to music school instead of the Ivies? Because music is too risky, according to my parents. They didn't come all the way from Korea so I could become a top-notch homeless violinist with no job and no health insurance. And even though I love playing my violin, I'm not good enough to be the next Sarah Chang. So why even consider music as a profession if you can't be Number One? That's why violin is my hook and not my future.

Chop chop chop.

Now I'm dicing the onions. They sting my eyes, and I try not to cry. I stare at the huge pile of wonton wrappers in the middle of the table and sigh. *Mandoo* are Korean potstickers stuffed with everything from cabbage to tofu to ground pork to bean sprouts to onions to eggs. Making *mandoo* is an endless process— you dip your fingers into the bowl of water and spread the water around the edge of a wonton wrapper. Then you spoon up some of the ground mixture and place it in the dry center. Then you fold, pinching the edges together to seal everything in, and dust flour over it.

It's easier than it sounds, but so far this morning, I've been able to make only three *mandoo*, and they're far from perfect compared to the 150 hermetically sealed *mandoo* my mom has made. My edges aren't scalloped as evenly, and sprouts poke through the sides because I keep puncturing the wonton wrapping with my nails every time my mom breaks my concentration by yelping, *"HARVARDYALEPRINCETON."*

My mom sets the sliced cabbage aside and dips her fingers into the wet mixture of sautéed meat, sprouts, and scrambled egg. She scoops up the perfect amount and places it exactly in the center of the wonton skin. I marvel at her precision, probably honed from all the weighing and measuring she does at the Avalon Health Center, where she is a pharmacist. My *mandoo* look pathetic next to hers.

"You should sign up for more SATs," my mom says. "When can you take them again?"

"January," I say.

She sighs. "That's so far away." Then she smiles. "At least this will give you plenty of time to do better."

I finish dicing the onions and set them aside. I'm about to start spooning more ground pork mixture onto an empty wonton skin to make the best *mandoo* ever when I notice the roar of the lawn mower has stopped.

My dad enters, waving the mail in the air. He's dressed in his Saturday uniform (gray sweatpants and Seoul National University sweatshirt), his hands covered with grease marks. He smells of freshly cut grass. Saturday's the one day when he's not working at the office or hunched over his computer at home, designing and building software systems for banks and insurance companies. So what does he do on his one day off? He fixes things. He likes to spend Saturday taking care of all the work around the house—mowing the lawn, patching the roof, fiddling with the car engine. He hates it when things don't work.

He hands me a thick manila envelope. The return address says, "Connecticut Music Festival Association."

"Looks like All-State results," he says.

"This is the most important All-State because of the concertmaster solos," my mom adds. (What, me get pressure from my parents? *Naah.*)

I rip open the envelope and yank out the music sheets for the *Capriccio Espagnol* and the first movement of Dvořák's *New World* Symphony, no. 9. I immediately look at the right-hand corner for the seating assignment. The first word indicates the instrument; the first number, the Roman numeral, indicates the "desk" or stand designation; and the second number indicates your chair. (Each music stand is shared by two people.)

18

For three years, it's always been "FIRST VIOLIN, I-1." First stand, first chair outside. Concertmaster.

I glance at the upper right-hand corner. For the first time, I see "FIRST VIOLIN, I-2." First stand, second chair inside. I won't play the violin solos from the Rimsky-Korsakov and I won't lead the violin section because I'm the . . .

Assistant concertmaster.

You gotta be kidding me. Okay, I know it wasn't my best audition, but how badly did I screw this up? I don't mean to brag, but frankly, my worst violin playing is usually someone else's best.

Oh no. Cute Trumpet Guy. It's all his fault. If he hadn't distracted me, I would be looking at "FIRST VIOLIN, I-1" stamped across my music instead. I can't believe I let a guy—cute or not—prevent me from getting concertmaster. He blew my winning streak!

My parents look at the music and immediately switch to Korean. My shoulders stiffen as their voices rise. "Well, I was already concertmaster for three years in a row," I say, trying to make light of this nightmare scenario. "Assistant concertmaster's still pretty good— it's like I won second place."

Silence from my parents. Because there's no such thing as SECOND PLACE. You're either FIRST or LAST. In fact, anything below First Place is a disgrace. My parents raised me to believe that Second Place is simply a polite way of saying "First Place for Losers." Of course, my parents' expectations clash with today's whole touchy-feely New Age positive reinforcement philosophy of "We're All Winners!" No way, according to my parents. Not all of us are winners. If we were, then *HARVARDYALEPRINCETON* wouldn't exist.

"At least I'm still sitting in the first desk," I say, trying to salvage my pride. Tears fill my eyes. It must be from all those onions I just chopped.

"But everyone will know you're not the best," my dad says.

"Uh rim up su," my mom says, sniffing. *(It's not even close.)*

DISCLAIMER: I don't speak fluent Korean. Why? My parents were afraid I might grow up speaking English with a Korean accent. They very rarely even talk about their lives in Korea. All I know is that they studied all the time, never drank alcohol, and never went to parties. My dad once told me that the SATs were nothing compared to the infamous exams that all Korean high-school graduates had to take to determine their futures. Anyway, they speak English all the time, with the exception of a few phrases. So I have the vocabulary of a four-year-old when it comes to speaking Korean, stuff like "I'm hungry" and "I have to pee." The only other words I'm familiar with are the following phrases:

어림없어
(Uh rim up su)
This basically means "It's not even close" or "No competition."

아직안되
(Ah jik an dae)
"Not yet acceptable."

만족못해
(Man jok mot hae)
I get this one all the time—"Not satisfactory" or "Not good enough."

"You should still practice the solos," my dad says.

"Why?" I ask. "I'm not performing them."

"But you should be ready in case the concertmaster gets sick," he says.

Suddenly the idea of a sick concertmaster and me taking over his/her seat to save the day pleases my mom, who starts smiling again. She puts down the music and scoops more meat and cabbage onto an empty wonton wrapper.

I reach for a wrapper. My mom places her hand over mine. "I'll finish these," she says. "You should go upstairs and take another practice test."

"But Susan and I are going to the movies later."

"What's more important, movies or SATs?"

I hate to admit it, but my mom's got a point. Susan will understand, especially after I tell her my scores.

Meanwhile, my parents are still discussing my disgraceful SAT scores, acting as if I've already left the kitchen. "Patti needs more help with the word problems . . ." "She has trouble with the geometry section . . ." "We should buy her another SAT practice book . . ." "Which SAT book is better, the Princeton

Review or Barron's?" "I don't know . . . why don't we get both?" "Good idea!"

I shake the flour from my hands. I gather the All-State music together. I glance at the list of all the members of the All-State Orchestra. The first side is everyone who made it into the brass and woodwind sections. The string players' names are on the other side. I wonder who is listed as Concertmaster. But before flipping the paper over, I notice the trumpet section.

Principal Trumpet: Diane Young
Associate Trumpet: David Petring
Trumpet III: John Fullerton
Trumpet IV: Ben Wheeler

I don't recognize any of these names. But what if Cute Trumpet Guy is among them? Oh my God, I can't believe I'm thinking about him again. I remember the way he stood so tall and straight as he played the trumpet, how tiny lines crinkled at the corners of his eyes when he smiled at me, and how his fingers lightly brushed against mine as he handed me my sheet music.

I shake my head. Focus, Patti! I don't have time to daydream about a cute guy I won't even see again until April. I shove the paper back inside the envelope and go upstairs.

Practice SAT Test #3

SAT TIP OF THE DAY: Do not cut corners if you are stressed for time. You will find questions with wrong answers specifically created to exploit a test taker's misunderstanding when worried about the time factor.

Select the lettered word or set of words that best completes the sentence.

1. Her scholarly rigor and capacity for _____ enabled her to undertake research projects that less _____ people would have found too difficult and tedious.

(A) fanaticism . . . earnest

(B) comprehension . . . indolent

(C) avarice . . . generous

(D) negligence . . . dedicated

(E) concentration . . . disciplined

Okay, so I know the answer is E. The girl in this sentence is full of "scholarly rigor" so obviously the first blank should have a word that is complementary to "rigor." That would be "concentration." And people who would find her research project too "difficult and tedious" would be less "disciplined" than her.

Then again, I don't think "less disciplined" is a very nice thing to say about people who find things difficult and tedious. Maybe they're just having a bad day. Maybe they found out they were assistant concert-master, too, or . . .

Stop wasting valuable test-taking time! I pick up my pencil and fill in the blank circle next to (E) concentration . . . disciplined.

. . . Wait a second. Now I'm looking at (C) avarice . . . generous. That makes no sense at all in this sentence completion. I know every word in the dictionary, thanks to last spring's SAT boot camp where we had to memorize fifty vocab words each week. According to the dictionary, avarice means "an unreasonably strong desire to obtain and keep money."

You know, I seriously question the dictionary folks for their closed-minded, judgmental attitude toward one's desire for money. What makes that desire "unreasonably strong"? Like it's a crime to want to make a lot of money? What if your parents are Korean immigrants who work really hard so they can save up enough money to pay the tuition for HYP?

I check my watch. Ten minutes have gone by. Oh no. According to my SAT prep course book instructions, I'm supposed to spend no more than a few minutes on each question. I slam the book shut. There's no way I'll finish this test in time. Besides, I've already taken SAT Practice Test #1 and #2 and I'm exhausted. I need a break.

I lean over and open the bottom drawer of my desk. I pull out a giant folder filled with all my math tests, starting from the seventh grade. My dad makes me collect them for future reference. But hidden between the Algebra II and Trigonometry tests is the latest issue of *TEEN POP!* magazine I've managed to sneak into the house. The older issues are hidden in a box stashed in the corner of my closet. *TEEN POP!* has a website, but I prefer their magazine because of the huge foldout posters stapled inside.

DISCLAIMER: Let me state now that I think *TEEN POP!* is pretty bad. The articles have too many exclamation points !!! about the Hottest 21 Stars Under 21! And the Annual Top Ten Cutest Rockers!! And the Most Eligible Hollywood Hottie Bachelors! Please. There's only one reason why I buy *TEEN POP!* every month.

Jet Pack.

I know, it's embarrassing, but let me explain. Last October my church youth group was really burned out from midterms. We turned on the TV in the rec room and ended up watching MTV all afternoon. And that's how I discovered Jet Pack. MTV played their video "Call It Love." I fell in love immediately. The lead singer/guitarist had long bangs that covered his eyes, pouty lips, and this gravelly voice. The other band members were equally gorgeous. I could not get the song or the video out of my head for the rest of the day. Instead of doing my trig problems later, I spent all night on my computer, searching for Jet Pack photos and websites online and downloading all their songs onto my iPod.

Jet Pack is from England. The lead singer, Simon Taylor, started the band during his first year at Cambridge. They were signed to Virgin Records two years later, dropped out of the university, and have been touring ever since. Their second album is coming out this fall. I can't wait! I think they sound like a cross between Radiohead and U2. (Well, except their lyrics aren't that intelligent or political . . . they mostly sing about why a girl just broke their heart and how sorry they are.) Rock critics make fun of them, especially because most of their fans are thirteen-year-old girls. But I don't care.

I look at the cover of *TEEN POP!* I never read the entire magazine, only the Jet Pack articles and photos. They were on the cover last month, so this time there's only a small photo of Simon Taylor on the upper right-hand corner. The headline next to Simon's head shouts: *"Baby pictures inside!"*

The baby pictures of Simon are pretty blurry—but wow! He is *so* cute! Here's a photo of Simon at age eleven, standing on a swing. Oh wow—Simon's hair was blond when he was a kid! He always dyes it a different color. My favorite? Burgundy.

If they ever had an SAT test on Jet Pack, I'd easily score a perfect 2400. Ask me anything. Rhythm guitarist Nick Isaac is five feet nine although some magazines claim he's five feet eleven, and he's the son of a fisherman and was raised in the fishing village of Cullercoats near Tynemouth. The bassist, Andy Rogers, likes to read biographies while on the road touring with the band. Drummer John Bates was born on October 27 in Paris, where he lived for ten years before moving back to England with his family, and he speaks fluent French.

Although I love each member of Jet Pack equally, if I was forced to choose only one, it would have to be Simon Taylor. He was born Nigel Simon Taylor in Birmingham, England, on August 20. He just turned twenty-three years old.

Out of nowhere Cute Trumpet Guy's face appears in my mind. What is my problem? I can't stop thinking about him. Even though his hair is brown, not burgundy, he kind of looks like Simon Taylor with his thin nose and angular chin. And when you think about it, Cute Trumpet Guy is a musician just like Simon. I remember how long Cute Trumpet Guy's bangs were, how they covered his eyes, and how he had to push them away in order to see me.

My mom knocks on the door, scaring me. "Patti? Are you done?" She tries to open the door, but I have it locked. She bangs on the door. "Patti?"

I shove the magazine into the drawer, accidentally ripping the cover almost in half. Great. I shut the drawer. I rush to the door and let my mom in.

"I just started the sentence completion section," I say quickly. "I locked the door so I could time myself."

The suspicious look in my mom's eyes disappears, replaced with regret for having ruined my practice SAT session. "I'm sorry," she says. "I'll leave you alone."

"Okay," I say, acting as casual as possible.

"Good girl." She leaves. I shut the door and sigh. That was a close call. I better finish taking this SAT test. But I have to look at Simon one last time. I pull out the magazine again and flip to the last page of *TEEN POP!* It features another photo of Simon Taylor and the headline "Next month: 10 Things You Never Knew About Simon Taylor!" I. Can't. Wait. Practice SAT Test #3 or no Practice SAT Test #3, at least I have something to look forward to.

How to Make Your Korean Parents Happy, Part 2

Attend Korean church every week, no matter what.

Church Is Cool!

The grilling is endless. I just told everyone that I didn't make concertmaster.

"Hey, you're just giving someone else a chance at first chair," says Tiffany Chung, her voice dripping with fake sympathy because she also plays violin and sits behind me in youth orchestra.

"That audition was fixed," Samuel Kwon says, surprising me with his righteous indignation on my behalf. "Screw them."

"Don't say *screw*," Kyung Hee Park snaps.

She's got a point. After all, we're in church. It's 12:30 on Sunday afternoon, and service at the

Woodward Korean United Methodist Church ended at 11:45 A.M. After service, everyone goes to the Fellowship Hall and greets each other. Lunch starts at 12:30, and that's when we all split up for the afternoon activity hour. We church youth group members grab paper plates stockpiled with rice, kimchi, *bulgogi*, *chapchae* noodles, and my mom's *mandoo*, and head for the rec room, where we sit on folding chairs in a semicircle. The adults remain in Fellowship Hall for Adult Bible Study while the little kids are hustled back to the Sunday School classroom.

Anyway, the whole "You're not concertmaster?" conversation started when our church youth group leader, Kyung Hee, announced the annual Spring Lock-In would be on the second Saturday of April.

I had raised my hand and said I couldn't participate because that was the same date as the All-State Orchestra concert. Which prompted Kyung Hee to say, "Of course, we can change the date because you're the All-State concertmaster." Which then led to me having to say the dreaded words: "Actually, I'm assistant concertmaster this year."

The long, awkward silence that followed made me

wish I had said something less dramatic, like "I have six months to live."

See, it's bad enough that I have to deal with my parents harping on my SAT scores and the pressure to get into *HARVARDYALEPRINCETON*. But I also have to deal with . . . Korean church.

Korean church is not just a place where Korean families congregate to celebrate God and socialize with each other. Korean church is also where parents try to one-up each other on their children's accomplishments. They all pretend that they don't approve of bragging— but somehow they manage to list everything their child has done while still sounding like humble Christians.

Let's take Tiffany Chung, a senior at Miss Porter's School in Farmington. Straight As, nailed a 2300 on the SATs the first time she took them. "I don't know how she does it," Mrs. Chung told my mom. "She works *so* hard but is *so* nice, never gets tired, always pleasant, smiling. Jesus tells us love one another, and Tiffany is always so pleasant, she loves everyone, even though she takes seven AP honor classes this year, she has so much homework but she gets straight As and she's so quiet, never brags about it, *so* modest, my Tiffany, oh, and Jesus is good."

And then there's Samuel Kwon, who attends Kingswood Oxford School in West Hartford, plays the cello (and has been principal cellist of All-State four years in a row), and is captain of their math team. But he's not perfect, according to his father, who told my dad, "Samuel had trouble with partial differential equations and variational calculus, so he worked hard and won a full scholarship to attend Yale's precollege math challenge program over the summer. It's a very difficult program to get into, oh, and praise Jesus."

James Ryu is a National Merit Scholar at Hall High. He also skipped two grades.

Lisa Kang is president of the National Honor Society at Farmington High and a nationally ranked fencer.

Sally Kim, a senior at the Ethel Walker School in Simsbury, won last year's Siemens Competition in Math, Science, and Technology (and was a finalist for two years in a row before that).

Isaac Rhee is captain of Avon Old Farms School's academic decathlon team, and they've won the state title every single year except his freshman year, because some school in Danbury beat them on a question about the contributions of the Corps of Discovery to the Lewis and Clark Expedition of 1804–6.

And then there's me. Patti Yoon—three-times-in-a-row All-State concertmaster, Greater Hartford Youth Orchestra concertmaster, National Merit Scholar, Honor Society, future valedictorian of my senior class at Woodward High (unless I get an A minus in AP calc, and then Susan Summers, my best friend, will take my spot because we're only 0.005 points apart in our GPAs), and winner of last year's Connecticut Young Artists Concerto Competition.

Of course, this is just the tip of the iceberg. We're all applying to the same Ivy League schools; hence we're not as friendly around each other this year. (You don't need to know about anyone else in our church youth group, because they're not seniors—they're only underclassmen.)

Anyway, we're back to square one regarding the Lock-In. We need a new date. The Lock-In is our annual event where you bring a friend who doesn't go to church in order to show him or her why *church is cool!* I always invite Susan, my only friend at Woodward, and for some odd reason, she really gets a kick out of hanging out with my church youth group. Everyone brings a sleeping bag and a change of clothes. The church provides us with movie rentals, board games, books, and all the pizza and ice cream we can stuff down. We get "locked in" the rec room from noon Saturday through noon Sunday, and we basically stay up most of the night gossiping, playing games, and watching movies. Then Kyung Hee or one of the other adult supervisors leads a short Bible study discussion. The goal is to convince our heathen friends that yes, church *is* cool.

Kyung Hee pulls out her calendar. "How about February? Valentine's Day weekend is open. Let's vote—all in favor for Lock-In on Valentine's Day?"

There's a moment of silence as everyone slowly looks around, wondering if anyone here actually has a boyfriend or girlfriend and will refuse to vote. No one protests. So one by one, we all raise our hands.

"It's settled," Kyung Hee says. "Lock-In in February. I'm sure we can come up with some fun Valentine themes for this one."

"We could decorate the room in red," Isaac says.

Kyung Hee snaps her fingers. "That's a fun idea!"

"We could rent a bunch of romantic comedies," Sally offers.

Kyung Hee smiles. "That's a great suggestion!"

Everyone starts speaking at once, each person coming up with an even more imaginative idea than the previous one. Figures—it's just church youth group, but the competitive urge fills everyone's veins as they compete with each other to win Kyung Hee's approval for the Best. Lock-In. Activity. Suggestion. Ever.

I kind of zone out, not interested in participating. Sometimes, I admit, the church youth group sessions can be fun. I love Game Night, when we play everything from Pictionary to Trivial Pursuit to Charades. Okay, so it's really Bible Pictionary, Bible Trivial Pursuit, and Bible Charades, but despite the subject matter, the games themselves are really fun. I mean, you only have *thirty seconds* to draw something that resembles Joshua and the Battle of Jericho. I'm currently the reigning champ of Bible Pictionary. But I think activities like Lock-In take church youth group just a bit too far—why would I want to spend twenty-four hours with people I've known since kindergarten, locked up in the rec room of the church?

I wonder if Cute Trumpet Guy goes to church and if he likes things like Lock-In and . . . Come *on*.

"Earth to Patti!"

Kyung Hee's voice startles me and I accidentally knock over my plate, spilling rice all over the floor.

"Is everything all right?" she asks. "You look stressed."

"I'm not," I snap, getting down on my knees to pick up the food.

Kyung Hee frowns. "Patti, I can tell you're stressed. But remember, you come to church to find peace in *Jesus*." She smacks her forehead with an exaggerated move. She's very dramatic—she always plays the lead in our annual Christmas pageant talent show. She's also perfect—she's got flawless skin, thick glossy long hair, the "good" eyes (double eyelids so she can wear eye makeup the normal way—some Koreans, like me, don't have that extra fold above the eye, but more on that later), *and* she graduated summa cum laude from Princeton and just got her J.D. from Yale Law School. She's what I call the P.K.D. Perfect Korean Daughter. (Yeah. I hate her.)

She places two fingers against the corners of her mouth and lifts them upward to a smile. Her perfectly

41

white teeth blind me. "Remember? Think *positive*. You haven't participated yet—everyone's already come up with such great ideas for this year's Lock-In. How about you?"

I think fast. The sooner I can come up with an idea, any idea, the sooner she'll leave me alone. I say the first words that pop into my brain: "How about a scavenger hunt?"

To my surprise, Kyung Hee claps her hands in delight while everyone in the room glares at me. "That's *wonderful*," she practically shouts, her cheeks flushed. "You'll be in charge of coming up with a list of items for the scavenger hunt. Won't that be fun?"

Oh no. What have I done? Before I can protest, Kyung Hee beams at me. "See, Patti?" she asks. "Isn't church cool?"

She's actually ecstatic. She is twenty-five years old. Shouldn't she be doing twenty-five-year-old things, like, I don't know, dating? But she looks so happy that I can't bring myself to hurt her feelings by saying something like "Are you *insane*?" Instead I grit my teeth, smile, and force myself to say, "Yeah. Church is cool!"

I figure, while I'm aiming for *HARVARD-YALEPRINCETON*, it can't hurt to aim for Heaven, too.

42

How to Make Your Korean Parents Happy, Part 3

Don't talk to boys.[2]

[2]They will distract you from your studies. As a result, your grades will plummet and you will not be accepted into *HARVARDYALEPRINCETON*.

Beauty Fades and Stupid Is Forever

Oh *crap*. I've got gym first period.

I can't *believe* I have gym first period. I'm heading toward homeroom from the guidance counselor's office, where I just picked up my semester schedule, and I'm reading my list of classes.

1st	period:	Gym
2nd	period:	AP English
3rd	period:	AP Latin IV
4th	period:	AP calculus
Lunch		
5th	period:	AP physics
6th	period:	AP psychology
7th	period:	AP economics

The thought of having to start every day off with an hour of Coach Turner shouting at me to run faster and the girls rolling their eyes as I miss hitting the volleyball/basketball/field hockey/fill-in the-blank ball makes me want to go home and crawl into bed. Or stick hot pokers in my eyes. Whatever's less painful.

It's 7:45 A.M. I don't have enough time to swing back to my locker for my gym clothes. I'll have to race for it after the homeroom bell rings. I glance at my schedule. Senior Homeroom (T–Z) is in room 300. Great. That's at the other end of the school.

I'm out of breath by the time I reach homeroom. Everyone's talking and laughing and no one notices as I enter, my cheeks flushed, sweat trickling down my back. Our homeroom teacher, Ms. Fuller, points to the farthest chair in the far right corner. "Just in time, Patti," she says. "Your seat is there." I skulk over to my desk and sit down, trying to catch my breath.

And that's when he enters. Cute Trumpet Guy.

Oh. My. God. Now I *really* can't breathe. What's he doing here?

Ms. Fuller looks up at Cute Trumpet Guy. "Hello, and you are . . . ?"

45

"Ben Wheeler," he says. "Transfer student."

Ben Wheeler. His name is Ben Wheeler. I flash back to the names on the All-State list—Diane Young, David Petring, John Fullerton, Ben Wheeler. Cute Trumpet Guy got into All-State!

He hands a piece of paper to Ms. Fuller, who reads it and then points toward me. "Your seat is there."

The seat in front of me is empty. Every other seat is filled. Wheeler. Yoon. Ms. Fuller is seating us in alphabetical order. Ms. Fuller is the greatest teacher ever. I quickly run my fingers through my hair, smoothing the tangles out.

Ben "Cute Trumpet Guy" Wheeler walks down the aisle. He's taller than I remember, and he's wearing black jeans, a pair of black Chuck Taylors, and a T-shirt featuring four snarling guys and the words *The Clash* above them. I notice how muscular his arms are. (What am I doing? Stop staring. He'll think you're some crazy stalker girl.) I duck my head and look away as he eases into the seat in front of me, his long legs stretching out from underneath the desk. I concentrate on the word HELL etched across my desk. It's very

46

lightly scratched in, probably with a nail file, the letters sharp and angular. I trace the H, then the E, the L . . .

"I know you."

I look up, my finger still tracing the final L in the word. Ben Wheeler has turned around and is staring right at me. His hair is shorter and his bangs no longer cover his eyes. He must've had his hair cut before the first day of school, but it still curls behind his ears. His face is thinner than I remember, and his nose is slightly crooked. But somehow, these imperfections make him even more perfect. He lays his hand on my arm briefly and says my name. "Patti Yoon."

His palm feels so warm against my arm. The room spins. I feel dizzy.

He says my name again, this time in the form of a question. "Patti Yoon? All-State?"

I realize I should say something. "Yes."

"Yeah, I remember you from the auditions. I'm Ben."

Silence. Come on, Patti, think of something clever to say, something to show off your razor-sharp wit and brilliant verbal acuity.[3] (Look, I memorized five hundred

[3]Acuity (noun) "Keeness of hearing, sight, or intellect."

47

SAT verbal words during last spring's SAT boot camp, so I gotta use them somehow!)

"Hi." Pause. "Ben." That's it? That's all I can come up with, Miss "At Least I Got a 700 in Critical Reading" Yoon? (Please, please don't blurt out "acuity.")

"So how'd you do on your audition?" he asks, unaware of my internal agony. "Did you get good news?"

"I'm assistant concertmaster." I wince at the word *assistant*.

"That's great! You must be amazing." He's actually impressed. For a moment, being assistant concert-master doesn't seem that awful. The look on his face is that of pure admiration. I melt.

"How did you do?" I ask, even though I already know the answer.

"I got fourth trumpet," he says. "My first time in All-State. I'm surprised I even got in. I've only played trumpet for a few years. Guitar's my main instrument."

There's something so easy and laid-back in Ben's tone that I relax, forgetting about All-State. I want to know as much as I can about Ben. "How long have you played guitar?" I ask. I can't believe I'm talking to a really cute guy and for the first time ever *it's not about his math homework.* I love that we share music in common. It makes it easier to talk to him.

"Since the second grade."

"What kind of music?"

"I started out with jazz, but I also play rock and the blues on my electric guitar."

"What bands do you like?"

He points to his shirt. "Old-school stuff. My dad got me into them. Ramones, Black Flag, Iggy Pop and the Stooges, MC 5, The Clash—"

"I love The Clash!" I say a little too quickly. I've never heard of The Clash. (Note to self: Google The Clash as soon as you get home.) I wonder if he likes Jet Pack.

Ben leans over and points to my class schedule. "All APs? What are you, a brainiac?"

Oh no. I cover my schedule with my arm. He smiles. Oh my God. His smile is so beautiful, so perfect. His teeth are perfect. Tiny lines crinkle at the corners of his green, green eyes. He is so cute that it hurts to look at him.

"I don't know how I'm gonna handle all these classes this semester," he says, waving his schedule in front of me. I realize he doesn't care that I'm taking all AP classes. "And I've got cross-country in the fall, then track in the spring."

"You run?"

"Yeah, I was captain of the track team back in Birmingham."

Jet Pack is from Birmingham, England. That photo of Simon Taylor with his long burgundy-dyed bangs covering his eyes flashes before me.

"Birmingham?" I ask, confused. "In England?"

He smiles. "No, Michigan." He holds up his left hand and points to the middle of his palm. "It's right here. Oh, sorry, that's what everyone does in Michigan to show where they're from. You know, the state's shaped like a mitten." He grins. "I'm talking your ear off, huh?"

At this point Ben could simply recite all the names and numbers from the phone book, and I would still be happy.

Someone snorts. I manage to look away from Ben for one second, and I notice three girls in homeroom are staring at us.

Stephanie Thomas sits right in front of Ben. To her

right, Maura Templeton. Next to Maura, Erin Warner. The three most popular and athletic girls in my high school. Maura and Erin both have long, layered brunette hair and are pretty in that vaguely spunky-supporting-actress-role-on-a-TV-sitcom kind of way. The only way I can tell them apart is that Erin's taller. Stephanie's got soft blond cotton-candy curls spilling past her shoulders. When I was in the ninth grade, I tried to curl my hair like hers, but my hair was so flat and stringy that I ended up tangling it instead and had to cut two inches off the knotted disaster. That was the year I decided that being pretty like Stephanie was never going to happen for me—the best I could do was to concentrate on my grades, because as they say, beauty fades and stupid is forever.

Stephanie, Maura, and Erin are whispering and pointing at us. I hear a few words, something like "What's he doing . . ." and "Why her . . . ?"

All at once, I get it. Ben, with his lean legs and wavy brown hair and nervous smile, former captain of his high-school cross-country team in Michigan . . . Oh crap. He's a jock. He's one of *them*—i.e., the A-Tier, the Popular Kids, the Beautiful People, the Plastics.

In other words, he's *way* out of my league.

Suddenly, just as I realize this, he gazes in the direction of Stephanie as she slathers lip gloss over her already glossy rosebud lips. She's wearing a cropped sparkly tank top showing off her incredibly flat abs and tiny waistline, her slim legs clad in a pair of perfectly snug jeans from the Gap. From a purely academic standpoint, yes, Stephanie Thomas is beautiful, with her wide, expressive dark-blue eyes and cute, buttony, pert nose and heart-shaped face. She's so hot that she practically glows with this Hollywood radiance, even under the harsh glare of our homeroom's blinking fluorescent lights.

Ben leans forward, trying to get the best view possible. Stephanie has that effect on guys.

I flash forward to next spring, imagining Ben and Stephanie together at the prom in May, his arm wrapped around her petite waist, the two of them smiling for the camera with their perfect toothy grins and chiseled cheekbones. Then I picture myself standing behind them, me with my fat nose, broad face, chubby thighs, thick eyeglasses, and my flat, straight hair with those annoying flyaways forming a halo on top of my head. I hate it when I feel this way, because it makes all my straight As seem meaningless.

As I feel the life rush out of me, I notice how Ben is now starting to size me up, his nervous smile fading as he tries to find an out to our conversation so he can turn around and upgrade from Patti Version 1.0 to Stephanie Version 2.0, and how I'm now saying more words than him as he grows silent, our conversation fading.

The bell rings. Ben turns around. Ms. Fuller reads the morning announcements. It's hard to pay attention to her, because Stephanie, Maura, and Erin can't stop giggling. Stephanie leans over and taps Ben's hand. I'm shocked by her boldness. "Hi," she says. "I'm Stephanie."

"Ben." He smiles warmly at her, and I don't feel so special anymore.

She grabs his semester schedule and looks it over. "I have gym first period too!" she squeals, touching his arm again. His eyes light up. When he speaks, he suddenly sounds muffled and far away, as if speaking underwater.

"Cool," he says. "Do you know where the gym is?"

"Yeah," Stephanie says. "Stick with me. I'll show you the ropes."

Ms. Fuller finishes the morning announcements. The second bell rings for first period. Everyone rushes for the door. My schedule slips off my desk. I bend over to pick it up. When I look up, he's gone.

Newton's Third Law of Motion

Maura stands in front of our goal cage, pointing at me and screaming. I can't make out exactly what she's saying—it's either "Pass it to me!" or "Pass it to Erin!"

It's 8:40 in the morning. The bell for second period will ring at 8:55, which is, like, *fifteen billion* minutes from now. I contemplate tripping on purpose to sprain my ankle, but Coach Turner would probably make me goalie instead. She doesn't look like your typical gym teacher—she's actually this tiny sprite of a woman with a pixie haircut and wiry arms and legs, and I think she's like fifty years old. She's always fluttering on the sidelines like some manic Tinkerbell, shouting out positive-yet-vague slogans, like "Never give up!" and "You can do it!" Coach Turner is all about overcoming obstacles and building character. For example, she always makes me captain when it comes to assigning opposing teams for whatever sport we're about to learn. She does that because I'm the worst athlete in the school, and she doesn't want me to be chosen last all the time. Coach Turner is all about building self-esteem.

Coach Turner wouldn't last a day in Korean church.

Right now, I'm stuck somewhere between Dante's eighth and ninth circles of Hell—this is that special area of brimstone and fire reserved for people like me who hate field hockey, a cardinal sin at Woodward High, where our girls' varsity field hockey team has won the last five Class M state championships in a row. I clutch my hockey stick and look around hopelessly. Where is the stupid ball? How can anyone find something so small in all this grass?

Maura shouts again. "Patti! It's over there! See? There! There! Right *there*!" Maura is not known for her verbal acuity.

I turn to see where "there" is. *Bam!* Stephanie runs right into me. Her hair is pulled back in a tight ponytail, and I swear I can see a vein pulsing in the middle of her shiny forehead. And then—*Whack!* Her field hockey stick slams against my left knee.

I stumble. Tears sting my eyes. The skin around my knee smarts, turning purple. Will this be an intramuscular or periosteal bruise? (Hey, I got an A in AP bio; when else am I gonna use this info?)

I want to throw down my stick and quit.

Suddenly I spy the ball. It's lying just two feet from me. Stephanie charges past it. Erin runs around in circles, trying in vain to find the ball.

Across the field, the guys in our gym class are playing soccer. I spot Ben in the distance. I wonder if he can see me.

You know what? Forget quitting. Stephanie may be captain of the girls' varsity field hockey team and I may be the worst field hockey player in the world, but *I saw the ball and she didn't.* I can beat her. I know I can. And maybe, just maybe, Ben will look up and see me strike the ball into the goal cage, scoring one for my team.

I blink away the tears and ignore the throbbing pain in my left leg. I grip my stick and aim for the ball.

Take your time, Patti. Remember your science classes? Just think of Newton's Third Law of Motion: "There is an equal and opposite reaction for every action." In other words—hit the ball. The rest will work itself out somehow.

F=MA, I think as I smack the ball as hard as I can. Force equals Mass times Acceleration. That's Newton's Second Law of Motion.

The ball flies in the air, past Stephanie's awestruck expression and toward the goal cage and . . .

Oh no. The ball continues past the goal cage and over the boundary lines to the other side of the field, where the guys are playing soccer. This is Newton's First Law of Motion—the law of inertia, which says an object in motion will continue moving until some external force stops it.

That external force turns out to be Ben. The ball hits him in the back.

Coach Turner blows her whistle. Everyone stops. Ben turns and—of course—chooses this moment to notice me. I should be mortified, but instead I'm relieved that he's still standing.

Stephanie jogs over. She points in my direction

and says something. Ben smiles, turns around, and looks for the ball. He finds it and throws it to her. The whistle shrieks again, and he sprints back into the boys' soccer game. He seems to float above the field, his feet a graceful blur.

Stephanie returns to our side of the field. She brushes past me, and I can't help but flinch as if she's about to hit me again with her stick. Stephanie smirks and mutters, "Chicken Patti."

And where is Coach "Positive Attitude" Turner when this happens? She's comforting Maura, who's still upset that I ruined the game. "I don't get it—I told Patti the ball was *there*."

It's so unfair. I hate gym. I hate field hockey. I hate Coach Turner. I hate Stephanie, Erin, and Maura.

To my incredible relief, the bell rings. I follow everyone to the locker room.

"Hey." I look up. Ben runs over. "Nice shot," he says.

"Nice what?" Oh. I get it. He's making fun of me. Suddenly I want to cry. This is so humiliating. "I'm so sorry I hit you," I say.

"I'm just kidding," he says quickly. "You've got a pretty strong arm, the way you hit that ball all the way over to where we were. Must be from all that bowing action on your violin?"

He's smiling as he says this. I can't believe it. He's not mad at me! I take a deep breath, blink back my tears, and smile my best I'm-not-as-pretty-as-Stephanie-but-at-least-I'm-smart smile. "Of course," I say, trying to imitate Stephanie's flirtatious tone. I toss my hair. My ponytail smacks me across the face. I pretend not to notice. "After all, I'm assistant concertmaster of All-State."

He laughs. "You're funny, Patti." And then he takes off.

Maybe having gym first period won't be so bad after all.

How to Make Your Korean Parents Happy, Part 4

1. Harvard
2. Yale
3. Princeton
4. Cornell
5. Dartmouth
6. Columbia
7. Brown
8. Penn
9. MIT
10. Stanford
11. University of California at Berkley
12. Smith/Mount Holyoke/Bryn Mawr/Wellesley[4]
13. Harvard or Yale Law School and/or Harvard or Yale Medical School[5]

---

[4]This is only for pretty girls like Tiffany Chung, whose parents will feel better if she attends an all-female Seven Sisters college because dating is wrong and evil.

[5]Law or medical school is the only way you can placate your Korean parents if you majored in something useless like English or philosophy during your undergraduate years.

14. When all else fails, marry a Korean doctor.
15. Become a Korean doctor.[6]

---

[6] Or better yet, combine 14 and 15.

The Pursuit of Excellence

The college applications arrived today. I'm in my room, flipping through the pages, each glossy brochure resplendent with eye-catching photographs of cobblestone courtyards, autumn foliage, ivy-covered brick buildings, and students lying on green campus lawns, reading Plato's *Republic* and looking extremely happy to be there.

Every single brochure has the phrase "The tradition of excellence" or "The pursuit of excellence" printed above those ivy-covered brick buildings and above those happy students reading Plato on the lawn.

I know how difficult the competition is to get into

the Ivy League. They accept only the cream of the crop. But then I read what is written inside each application form.

And I start to feel sick to my stomach.

Scary Harvard Statistics

Number of students who applied to **HARVARD**:
22,920

Number of students who were accepted:
2,131

Acceptance rate:
9.3%

Average SAT score:
2290

Students in the top 10% of their high-school class:
90%

Scary Yale Statistics

Number of students who applied to YALE:
19,060

Number of students who were accepted:
1,639

Acceptance rate:
8.6%

Average SAT score:
2265

Students in the top 10% of their high-school class:
95%

Scary Princeton Statistics

Number of students who applied to PRINCETON:
18,891

Number of students who were accepted:
1,927

Acceptance rate:
10.2%

Average SAT score:
2265

Students in the top 10% of their high-school class:
95%

Okay, So the Ivy League Can Bite Me

Total percentage of applicants accepted at **BROWN**:
13.8%

Average SAT score:
2225

Students in the top 10% of their high-school class:
94%

Total percentage of applicants accepted at **COLUMBIA**:
9.6%

Average SAT score:
2245

Students in the top 10% of their high-school class:
88%

Total percentage of applicants accepted at **CORNELL:**
24.7%

Average SAT score:
2175

Students in the top 10% of their high-school class:
87%

Total percentage of applicants accepted at
DARTMOUTH: 15.4%

Average SAT score:
2240

Students in the top 10% of their high-school class:
87%

Total percentage of applicants accepted at **PENN:**
17.7%

Average SAT score:
2225

Students in the top 10% of their high-school class:
91%

My Mom's Korean Spam Recipe #1 — Spam Bi Bim Bap

Ingredients:

1 can of Spam
1 jar of kimchee
Daikon radish–style kimchi
Spinach, cooked and drained
Bean sprouts
2 cups of steamed and cooked sticky rice[7]
1 egg
Bottle of *kochu jang* (Korean hot chili pepper sauce)
Toasted sesame seeds

Directions:

1. Slice Spam into thick French fry–style slices
   (ignore sick feeling in stomach as you grip the

---

[7] I grew up with a rice cooker, so if you want to know the directions on how to make sticky rice by using a regular pot of water, I can't help you. All I know is that you fill the rice cooker up with rice and water—simple math ratio of 2:1, two parts water to one part rice—cover it, and press the little button and wait until the red light goes off.

slick, gelatinous surface of the Spam). Fry the slices in a pan on the stove.

2. Let the cooked spinach cool and sprinkle with toasted sesame seeds.

3. Clean bean sprouts and cut off the tips. (This takes forever, so practice some SAT vocab words to pass the time.)

4. Place cooked rice in a giant bowl. Arrange spinach, bean sprouts, Spam, and daikon radish on the rice (I like to make mine look like a four-part pie chart).

5. Fry the egg and place it on top of the entire dish.

6. Pour on all the *kochu jang* sauce you want, mix it up, and eat with a side of kimchi. (Note: I'm assuming you have a local Korean grocery store somewhere in your town where you can buy the kimchi, daikon radish, and *kochu jang* sauce. If you don't, well, the only way to make kimchi is to ferment a bunch of cabbage underground for a few years. Good luck with that.)

7. Enjoy!

Koreans love Spam. There's something about those quivering jelly-covered slabs of pink-and-white marbled mystery luncheon meat that drives Korean people crazy. It's all America's fault—during the Korean War of 1950–53, American soldiers ate Spam all the time. The Koreans got curious, fried the Spam with some rice and kimchi, and the rest is history. Outside of the United States, Korea eats more Spam than any other country in the world. It's even considered a very classy gift to give to your loved ones over the holidays. I once read that South Korea spends $136 million on Spam every year.

$136 million. That's a lot of Spam.

Even though I'm totally one hundred percent American, every now and then this weird genetic anomaly in my body is activated and I find myself acting more Korean than American. Especially when it comes to Spam. I can't help it—I grew up on it and I love the stuff.

Blame it on my mom. She's been inventing Korean Spam dishes for as long as I can remember. When I was born, my mom was getting her degree at the School of Pharmacy at the University of Connecticut and my dad had just been hired to work for a software company in Danbury. We lived in an apartment outside the Storrs campus, and my parents were working overtime to save up their money for my future college fund, which they had established before I had even been born. Spam is cheap, so my parents ate a lot of it. I guess you could say Spam is the reason why my parents can afford to pay for any college I will attend.

My favorite recipe is my mom's Spam *bi bim bap*. *Bi bim bap* is a popular Korean dish featuring a bunch of seasoned vegetables and meat and a fried egg (don't ask) and this spicy Korean sauce called *kochu jang* served on top of sticky white rice. Except every now and then, my mom makes it with Spam. I had introduced this Spam dish to Susan when she had slept over at our house when we were younger. She was a little horrified, but not only did she end up loving my mom's Spam *bi bim bap* but she also requested a second helping. She asked my mom for the recipe, and today Susan makes a pretty mean Spam *bi bim bap* herself.

The only problem with Spam *bi bim bap* is that you can't eat it before school. It's because of the kimchi, a popular Korean side dish made of fermented cabbage with chili peppers. Koreans eat kimchi with *everything*. The kimchi stinks up your breath, and no matter how many times you brush your teeth, you can't get rid of the smell. So Spam *bi bim bap* has become a Saturday-morning tradition. (I don't worry about kimchi breath at orchestra rehearsal later that day, because half the orchestra is Korean anyway.)

My mom and I sit in the kitchen with our steaming bowls of Spam *bi bim bap*. I break the yolk with my fork and mix it together with the rice.

"May I have the soy sauce please?" I ask. My mom hands me the bottle. I shake several drops into my bowl. I know it sounds gross, but I swear, this stuff tastes *so good*. My stomach growls. I can't wait to eat. I dig up a healthy amount of egg, rice, Spam, and kimchi with my fork and am about to eat it when . . .

"I looked over the college applications," my mom says. "You have a lot of work to do. Don't procrastinate. You should select your essay topics later tonight."

My stomach twists. "Can we not talk about this right now?" I say. "I'm a little freaked out by them."

"But the essays are very important," she says. "You are a very strong essay writer. These essays can make or break you. Mrs. Kwon told us that the valedictorian at Samuel's school last year failed to get accepted into *HARVARDYALEPRINCETON* even though he had a perfect 2400 SAT score. His essays were terrible."

Great. Now I have to worry about writing an exceptional essay for my college apps. One more thing to add to my Top Ten Things to Do list. Suddenly I'm not only hungry, I'm *starving*. I start shoveling my mom's Spam *bi bim bap* into my mouth, barely chewing before I swallow. But no matter how much Spam rice I shove down my throat, it's not enough to fill the emptiness inside me.

How to Make Your Korean Parents Happy, Part 5

Don't rock the boat. Keep a low profile. Stay out
of trouble.

College Essay Question No. 1

> 1. Discuss some issue or event of personal,
>   local, national, or international concern
>   and its importance to you.

I don't know how it starts.

For the record, we do nothing to provoke this. Susan and I are just waiting in line at the cafeteria, minding our own business, when Eric Sanders and his friends approach us.

"Hey Susan," Eric says.

Susan and I exchange glances—this can't be good.

Eric Sanders is the quarterback of the football team and one of the most popular guys in our senior class. And for some reason, he's considered one of the cutest boys at our school, too—he's been on the Homecoming court since ninth grade. I don't understand what girls see in him—he may be tall and athletic, with thick, wavy reddish-brown hair and a spray of freckles across his face and a broad grin showing off pearly teeth, but there's this mean streak in his narrow eyes that throws his handsome features off kilter.

And Eric's mean streak comes out whenever he finds someone smaller or weaker than him to pick on. Namely me, Susan, and anyone who belongs to any after-school activity that doesn't involve organized sports.

"So, Susan," Eric says, smiling. "Wanna go to Homecoming?"

For one second, Susan's eyes flicker with hope. I know what she's thinking—*Hey, maybe this year Eric will be nice to me and realize that I'm much more than just Latin Club president.*

That flicker of hope is all Eric needs. "Then you should go," he says, cracking up. His buddies snicker.

Susan's shoulders slump. I'm not that impressed with Eric's punchline—he usually comes up with much more imaginative insults, like last year when he got everyone to call Susan the queen of the Hobbits because her feet are, well, for lack of a better term, big. (She's only a few inches taller than I am but wears a size nine shoe.)

I follow Susan down the line and grab a bowl of red Jell-O and a small salad. I wait for Eric to start picking on me next. Maybe he'll ask me to the prom, and then tell me to have a good time by myself.

Instead I hear the following words: "Ching chong ching ching chong."

What? *Ching chong ching ching chong?* I'm still trying to figure out the semantics behind this one as I wait for one of the cafeteria workers to hand over my lunch, which ironically is a chicken patty sandwich. Not that Eric would recognize irony even if it bit him in the butt.

I finally receive my chicken patty sandwich and head over to the cash register with Susan. Eric follows us, still muttering "Ching chong" under his breath.

"Ignore him," Susan whispers to me as she finishes paying for her lunch.

"That'll be three fifty," the woman at the register says.

"Chop chop," Eric mutters.

I'm about to pay for my sandwich when Eric says it. "Jap."

Oh my God. *I'm not Japanese!* Why is he even calling me a Jap? What does my ethnicity have to do with any of this? Why does Susan get to be called Queen of the Hobbits or dork or geek but I always get called Jap or Chink or gook? What does being Asian have to do with me being a nerd/geek/dork/physically uncoordinated loser? Why can't he just call me a geek, too? It would still hurt, but I'd take geek over gook any day. Because we all know geeks can change—just look at all those Hollywood romantic comedies where the girl geek takes off her glasses, unpins her ponytail, and turns into a princess. But I can't stop being Korean. I can't change my skin color. Even though I know he's wrong, Eric still makes me feel embarrassed for being Korean sometimes.

"Ah so," Eric says.

I can't take it anymore. *"Ah so"? I speak perfect English, you Neanderthal moron!* This is my senior year. I've got important college deadlines, SATs, class rankings, and All-State to worry about. I don't have time for Eric. I want to turn around and scream *"Shut up"* at him, but I'm too scared I might get in trouble. And my parents taught me not to rock the boat. Why? Any rabble rousing, political protesting, or subversive rebelling can lead to a potential detention, which could lead to a possible three-day suspension, which then gets recorded on your transcript, thus lowering your chances of getting into HYP. Although my parents have never specifically defined "rocking the boat," I assume that "standing up for yourself" counts. So I just stay here, silent, as Eric continues to make fun of us. I fantasize Eric will be one of those people who peak in high school, settling down at some cubicle in a boring dead-end clerical temping job while I—thanks to my Ivy League education—will own the company he works for. And then I will fire him.

But even though I have the maturity and the foresight to know that life is allegedly going to improve for me after graduation if I get into *HARVARDYALE-PRINCETON*, that knowledge is useless right here and now. I *still* have this year left of school. The future is still this gray mass of fuzzy nothingness, and all that matters is right now. Now is the only thing I can see clearly.

And now is when I decide not to pay for my chicken patty. I just walk away. Susan gasps. "Hey!" the woman at the register shouts. "You can't do that!"

But I just did. Once again, for the fourth year in a row, it's going to be another year of sneaking sandwiches into the library during lunch hour instead. I won't be going to the cafeteria, because I can't stand dealing with people like Eric Sanders making fun of me while I stand in line, waiting for my stupid chicken patty sandwich that's too dry and overcooked anyway.

Top Ten Koreans and Korean Americans Who Could Kick Eric Sanders's Butt[8]

1. Sarah Chang (Korean American Avery Fisher Prize–winning violin prodigy)
2. Margaret Cho (Korean American standup comic and star of the first ever all Asian American sitcom, *All-American Girl*)
3. King Sejong the Great (fifteenth-century Korean ruler who invented Hangul, the Korean alphabet)
4. Benjamin Lee (Korean University of Chicago theoretical physics professor who headed the theoretical physics department at the Fermi National Accelerator Laboratory)
5. Queen Min (forward-thinking nineteenth-century empress of Korea and political martyr)

[8]And one Korean Canadian: Sandra Oh (Golden Globe winner and Emmy-nominated actress)

6. Kim Dae-jung (former president of South Korea and Nobel Peace Prize winner)
7. Angela E. Oh (outspoken Korean American civil rights attorney and presidential adviser)
8. Michelle Wie (Korean PGA golf prodigy)
9. Chan Ho Park (Korean pitcher first signed to the Los Angeles Dodgers)
10. Hines Ward (his dad is African American and his mom is Korean and not only is he the NFL wide receiver for the Pittsburgh Steelers but he also helped his team win the 2006 Super Bowl and was voted Most Valuable Player)

$$(d/dx)\ 5\sin(x^2 + 1)$$

When you've got six AP classes, orchestra rehearsals, violin lessons, an upcoming solo concerto performance, All-State music to practice, college apps, *and* the SATs, you don't have time to waste. I have my Top Ten Things to Do Lists taped to my bathroom wall, reminders scribbled on my palm in blue ink, and home schedules updated on my computer every night before I go to bed.

And why do only one thing at a time? For example, during breakfast I will memorize ten SAT vocab words while eating my cereal. When I'm writing an English paper on, say, Jane Austen's *Pride and Prejudice*, I'll listen to my Sarah Chang Mendelssohn CD at the same time because it helps me memorize the notes.

Right now I've got ten minutes before the homeroom bell rings. Plenty of time to finish my extra-credit assignment for AP calc.

I zip through the first four problems. I'm about to start the final problem, $(d/dx) 5\sin(x^2 + 1)$, when Stephanie's voice breaks my concentration. "Hi Ben," she says.

Ben enters the room, his backpack slung casually over his right shoulder.

Even though school's been in session for two weeks already, my heart still skips a beat as I watch Ben maneuver his way through the maze of desks. He stops by Stephanie's desk. "Hey, Steph."

Steph? Since when did Ben have time to become so chummy with Stephanie? Why does my stomach feel all twisty and knotty right now?

But Ben doesn't stay by Stephanie's side. Instead he continues toward his seat. Stephanie's smile falters. She whips a compact mirror from her purse and bares her teeth, frowning at her reflection. My lips twist into a half smile.

"What's so funny?" Ben slides into his seat and leans toward me, his arm resting on my desk. He smells faintly of mint toothpaste. He glances at my assignment and smiles. "Oh. Calculus. Of course. That always cracks me up, too."

"The last problem's hilarious," I say sarcastically. "X-squared plus one, get it?"

"Stop it," he says, his tone equally dry. "You're killing me."

We laugh. I know, our jokes are kind of stupid, but it's not like we have a lot of material to work with—I usually have some extra-credit math assignment I'm working on, or a book I'm reading ahead in for class. It's become this little ritual since school started, the two of us kidding around before the bell rings. I don't know how long this will last before Ben figures out that associating with me will tarnish his popularity and reputation.

"Hey, what's that?" Ben points to the folder lying underneath my assignment.

"Just my math folder," I say, puzzled at his sudden interest in paper products.

"No, this." He pulls the paper sticking out of my folder.

Oh God. No! It's a picture of Jet Pack I cut out from *TEEN POP!* (I was planning to tape the picture in my locker.)

I want to die. I squirm as Ben hands the photo back. "I didn't know you liked Jet Pack," he says. A sly smile slowly spreads across his face.

My face feels hot. I'm so embarrassed, I can't even look him in the eye. "Yeah," I mumble.

To my surprise, Ben simply says, "That's cool. What other kinds of music do you like? I bet you love classical music, right? Who's your favorite composer?"

I can't believe Ben is interested in my musical tastes! "I don't have a favorite composer," I say. "But right now I'm studying Mendelssohn's violin concerto. It's a really beautiful piece."

"Mendelssohn." He tilts his head. "Never heard of him. The only classical stuff I know is the stuff everyone knows, like Bach and Mozart."

"That's a good start," I say. "I started off learning about them, too. . . ." My voice falters because Ben is staring directly into my eyes, acting as if I'm the only person in the room. He has this intense expression on his face, concentrating on my every word. I can't believe someone as good-looking and popular as Ben would be this interested in what I have to say. I glance quickly in Stephanie's direction. Even though her back is to me, I can tell that she's aware that Ben and I are having a deep conversation about something she knows nothing about. This makes me feel better. I straighten my shoulders and continue talking, no longer nervous. It is so easy to talk to Ben.

It's not until the bell rings and Ms. Fuller starts taking attendance that I realize I haven't finished the final problem on my extra-credit assignment. AP calc is during fourth period, and I won't have enough time between classes to finish solving $(d/dx)\ 5\sin(x^2 + 1)$. I won't be able to hand in the assignment on time, and therefore I won't get the extra credit. But for some reason, I don't really care.

Top Ten Reasons Why Sarah Chang Is Better Than I Am

1. Sarah Chang took violin lessons at Juilliard . . . at age five.
2. Three years later, Sarah Chang performed the Paganini Violin Concerto no. 1 with the New York Philharmonic.
3. By the fourth grade, Sarah Chang was practicing the violin three hours straight every day.
4. That same year, Sarah Chang also recorded her first album.
5. Sarah Chang made her Carnegie Hall debut at age seventeen.
6. The next year, Sarah Chang graduated from Juilliard.
7. Sarah Chang also won the prestigious Avery Fisher Prize from Juilliard.
8. Since then, Sarah Chang has performed all over the world with such famous orchestras as

the Berlin Philharmonic and the London Symphony.

9. Sarah Chang has also played with the most famous musicians in the world, including cellist Yo-Yo Ma and violist Pinchas Zuckerman.

10. And not only did Sarah Chang easily memorize the *entire* Mendelssohn concerto when she was my age, but she also recorded it with the Berlin Philharmonic.

College Essay Question No. 2

> 2. Describe an interest or activity that has
> been particularly meaningful to you.

The name David Oistrakh is scrawled at the top of my music. So are Sarah Chang, Itzhak Perlman, Joshua Bell, Isaac Stern, Kyung-Wha Chung, and Nathan Milstein.

These are the names of famous violinists who have all played Mendelssohn's Violin Concerto in E Minor. My violin teacher, Bernard Mishkind, wrote them down as suggestions for what recordings to listen to in order to inspire me to practice this piece.

I bought all their recordings. Each version of the Mendelssohn is different, depending on the violinist's style of playing. Sarah Chang's version is aggressive, while Itzhak Perlman's version is very refined and elegant. But no matter the style, they all have one thing in common—each version is brilliant.

Of course, instead of feeling inspired, I'm nervous. Especially right now as I play the first movement from memory for my teacher in his studio. It's Saturday morning, and I'm at the Hartt School for my weekly violin lesson.

I'm nervous because I haven't had enough time to practice. So instead of sounding like Sarah Chang, I sound like, well . . . My bow scrapes against the E string during the cadenza. It sounds about as pleasant as when my mom uses steel wool to clean the bottom of a frying pan. But it's not my fault. The violin is a very temperamental instrument. The slightest change in temperature or humidity can cause the glue between a violin's seams to dry out and create a crack in the wood. Sometimes dry weather can simply make your violin not sound as good as it usually does. Today's one of those days—no matter how hard I try, I can't seem to coax a warm-enough tone from the strings. Everything sounds harsh, especially when I hit the high notes on the E string.

I glance around the room. I've been coming to Mr. Mishkind's studio for the past five years. I auditioned for him in the eighth grade—I'm the youngest student he has ever agreed to teach. Although he's almost seventy years old and walks slowly across campus with the help of a cane, Mr. Mishkind plays the violin as if he's still a young man, his wizened, callused hands scampering up and down the fingerboard, producing a beautiful, rich sound.

I hit a flat note. Concentrate, Patti!

Despite my frustration, there's always this moment while I'm playing the violin when it no longer feels like I'm holding a violin in my hands. The instrument and the bow disappear, and all I can feel is the music. It becomes a part of me, and I become a part of it. This is my favorite part of playing the violin. Yeah, it's fun to show off my technical abilities and scare off my competitors. But sometimes it's just fun to enjoy the music. There's something about music that relaxes me and makes all the stress in my life disappear.

The piece ends sooner than I want it to—the last note fades away and I wait for Mr. Mishkind's critique. I'm sure he'll criticize my bowing on the triplets—they're really hard to play in tempo. That's the problem with the violin—as much as I love playing music, I want everything to be perfect. Making one tiny mistake can ruin my happiness when I play.

Instead, my teacher says something I wasn't expecting.

"You should apply to Juilliard," he says.

"Even though I messed up the triplets?"

"You can easily fix that." He opens a desk drawer. "You should play the Mendelssohn for your audition. Here." He hands over a manila envelope along with a shiny brochure. I open the Juilliard brochure to a page that says:

The Juilliard School seeks students who possess . . .
1. *Commitment to music training and a*
   career in music performance.
2. *Outstanding talent as a performer.*
3. *Personal maturity.*

I'm a good violinist, but do I really have "outstanding

talent"? Am I really that mature? Do I truly have a career in music performance? Am I really good enough to get into Juilliard?

"You're one of my top students," Mr. Mishkind says, interrupting my thoughts. "You have a very good chance of getting accepted into the best conservatories in the country."

I fight the urge to ask, "Who are your other top students?" and flip through the brochure. "But I'm still making mistakes in the cadenza," I say. "I'm not Sarah Chang."

"You don't have to be Sarah Chang to get into Juilliard," he says. "Don't worry. I'll give you some etudes to help fix your bowing problems with the triplets." He grabs a pencil and scrawls some bowing marks on my sheet music. "Think about applying," he continues. "The application and audition CD are due in late December. You should record the first two movements of the Mendelssohn concerto, the first movement of the Bach E Major Partita, and the Paganini Caprice no. 20. If you make the first cut, you'll be asked to do a live audition in March at the school."

"You're serious about this," I say, surprised.

But Mr. Mishkind seems even more surprised by my reaction. "I thought you were planning to go to music school," he says. "Patti, anyone can play the notes perfectly. But not everyone can feel the music the way you do. That's what makes you stand out from the other students. You play with your heart. You have a special gift. It would be a shame to waste it."

Gift? I have a gift? I never thought of my ability to play the violin as a gift. It was just something that came easy to me. I hear my mom shouting, *"HARVARD-YALEPRINCETON,"* in my head. There's no way my parents would even let me apply to Juilliard or any music school. They would say, "Music is too risky." I politely smile, shake my head, and say, "Juilliard is for serious musicians. I wasn't planning on majoring in music. It's just a hobby."

He puts the pencil down. "Are you sure?" he asks. "You already know most of the pieces required for the audition. We can review some of them at a future lesson if you decide to apply. You should also consider the Eastman School of Music and the New England Conservatory."

Great. Now Mr. Mishkind sounds like my mom, but instead of pressuring me to apply to the Ivies, it's to the top music conservatories in the country. Like I need more pressure about applying to college.

He points to my music. "You've got some time," he says. "For now, let's try these new bowings."

I put down the Juilliard application packet and pick up my violin. Right before I start playing, Mr. Mishkind says, "Patti, no matter where you apply for school, you should never give up the violin."

Give up the violin? Why would he say that? I have trouble concentrating and mess up the first line of the cadenza. So much for my gift. "Sorry," I say.

I play the cadenza again. I relax and let the music take over. Somehow my violin finally warms up and doesn't sound so tinny, the notes resonating from the wood. This cadenza is so beautiful and playful—I love how fun it is to play. As I get swept up in the notes, I think, Wait a minute. If I get into *HARVARDYALE-PRINCETON*, does that mean I don't have to play the violin anymore? If the whole point of studying the violin was in order to get accepted into the Ivy League, then what's the point of continuing to play the violin after I'm accepted? I could simply quit playing and let my violin collect dust in its case under my bed.

But I don't want to quit the violin. I've never thought about this before, and suddenly I can't imagine life without music, a future without my violin.

My fingers fly up and down the ebony fingerboard. I stare at my hands—they're small and childlike, and my fingers are really skinny. By themselves, my hands appear weak and defenseless. But when I'm holding my violin, my hands look strong and authoritative. And even though I'm now kind of confused about my future, the Mendelssohn concerto soothes me, the bright bubbling notes filling an empty space in my heart. As I near the end of the piece, I wonder: If I get into *HARVARDYALEPRINCETON* and quit studying the violin, will I still be happy?

The Challenge

Tiffany Chung raises her hand. "I do."

I want to scream. Tiffany Chung wants to challenge *me*?

It's noon on Saturday, and I'm at my weekly youth orchestra rehearsal. The Greater Hartford Youth Orchestra (GHYO) meets every Saturday from noon to three P.M. at the Hartt School of Music's Millard Auditorium. The GHYO is your typical youth orchestra where the best musicians sit in the top chairs.

I can't rest on my laurels as concertmaster of my youth orchestra, because we always have challenges. A challenge is when students test themselves and one another in a bid for a higher seat. If the challenge is successful, the student sitting in the higher seat has to move back and allow the other student to take his or her seat. Mr. Abraham Lurie, our conductor, always asks if anyone wants to challenge another player right before rehearsal starts.

Given that half of the Greater Hartford Youth Orchestra is made up of my Korean church youth group (Tiffany, Isaac, Sally, James, Samuel, and a whole bunch of juniors and sophomores), you can imagine how many challenges happen every week. But no one has ever dared to challenge me, because, well, no one would ever be able to beat me. Nonetheless, the past four years have been really tense, because I still have to be ready for a possible challenge every Saturday before rehearsal starts.

Of course, today is the first rehearsal that I have not had enough time to practice for. In addition to my Mendelssohn concerto, the Greater Hartford Youth Orchestra will also perform the Brahms Symphony no. 1 for our November concert. The Brahms has a huge concertmaster solo in the second movement. I sight-read it during last week's rehearsal. It's really beautiful, but it's hard hitting those high notes near the end.

And of course today is also the first time that someone decides to challenge me. Who? Tiffany Chung. Figures. She and I aren't the best of friends. We're polite to each other because our parents are friends, but we pretty much avoid each other during church and study group sessions. She's actually a pretty decent violinist, but technically there are some things she can't do as well as me. That's why I'm always seated ahead of her in orchestra and All-State.

I guess last week's sight-reading of the Brahms, when I mangled the last few notes, must have encouraged Tiffany to challenge me today. I refuse to look Tiffany in the eye as she stands up and walks across the stage to the conductor's podium.

"Please play the solo from the second movement of the Brahms," Mr. Lurie says, stepping down from the podium. Tiffany places her music on his stand. She raises her violin and plays.

Oh no. She sounds really good. She obviously practiced a lot. She hits all the notes in tune. The rhythm, impeccable. I hold my breath and . . . she doesn't miss any of the high notes.

When she finishes, the string players tap their bows

against their stands. That's the way orchestra members show admiration.

Mr. Lurie nods, clearly pleased with Tiffany's spotless performance. He waits as I stand up and head toward the podium. I glare at Tiffany as she walks past me.

I take a deep breath and raise my violin to my chin. To my surprise, my bow arm shakes. I never get nervous, and I never get stage fright unless I haven't practiced enough for a performance. Which is usually never . . . until today. That's because I'm not prepared for this challenge. The one and only time I have played this solo was when I sight-read it last week at our first orchestra rehearsal of the year. The Brahms Symphony no. 1 is considered one of the most difficult and challenging symphonies to play. Mr. Lurie told us it took Brahms twenty years to write his first symphony because he felt such pressure to live up to Beethoven's famous Ninth Symphony, the *Ode to Joy*. Pressure? Tell me about it.

I focus on an invisible point in the back of the orchestra hall, a trick I learned from Mr. Mishkind on how to calm your jitters. I've performed in this hall every year, from youth orchestra concerts to solo recitals.

This stage is my home away from home, with its worn-beige-carpeted aisles, squeaky wooden audience chairs, and purple curtains behind the stage. Somehow, all this comforts me and the fluttering in my stomach fades away. I sweep my bow across the strings. I make sure to play all the dynamic markings, from forte (loud) to pianissimo (very soft).

How could Brahms have written such a sublime melody under all that stress? It took twenty years for him to create this music. I'm in awe of how hard Brahms worked. Suddenly the beauty of this music takes over and I am no longer afraid of missing the high notes. I hit all of them in tune, using enough vibrato to give the notes warmth. I let the last note linger, my bow hovering above the strings for a moment before I relax and put down my violin.

It's very quiet. How bad was I? I look around, wondering why no one is tapping their bows against the stands. Did I really mess up? Then I stare at my feet, too nervous to look at anyone.

"That was . . . amazing," Mr. Lurie finally says. "Your ability to feel the music and play with emotion is remarkable."

I look up. He's smiling. Slowly everyone starts to applaud. I realize no one tapped their stands earlier because they didn't want to break the spell. Tiffany doesn't look happy, but she at least nods at me as if to say, Okay, you won.

"Patti can keep her seat," Mr. Lurie says as the applause dies out. "Tiffany, you did a wonderful job, but Patti will remain our concertmaster." He raises his baton. "Let's run through the first movement."

I raise my violin and wait for his cue.

How to Make Your Korean Parents Happy, Part 6

Be really, really, really good at math.

Hagwon

"The first step is to find the critical numbers," my dad says, scribbling away on a piece of scrap paper.

That's easy for him to say. Critical numbers? I don't even know what a number is anymore. My brain hurts so much that I want to reach inside my skull, pull it out, and tuck it into bed.

It's Sunday night, and we're sitting in the kitchen, going over my math homework. Every Sunday since I was six years old, my dad and I have sat at this same kitchen table, going over my math homework. It's a complex ritual, one in which my dad is in a good mood at first, excited to help me appreciate the wonderful world of numbers, and by the end of the night he's red in the face, shouting in frustration because my brain has shut down and I can no longer understand anything he's saying.

I'm actually a really good math student, but every now and then there's this odd disconnect in my brain that prevents me from grasping what are essentially simple concepts. For example, when I was in the fourth grade, learning how to calculate the area of a triangle took five hours. That remains the most traumatic Sunday night of my life, with my dad shouting, "Why can't you find the height of the triangle? It's so simple!" Today say the word *triangle* and I shudder.

But I have a feeling tonight's assignment may eclipse the epic Battle of How to Find the Height of a Triangle. I can't wrap my head around "The Constant Multiple Rule for Derivatives" ($d/dx \, c \cdot f(x) = c \cdot f'(x)$).

For the tenth time tonight, my dad slowly and patiently asks the question, "So the derivative of a constant times a function is the . . . ?"

It's like my dad is now talking in Korean—I don't understand a word he's saying. My shoulders hurt and I'm sleepy. Plus I can't stop thinking about what Mr. Mishkind said about applying to Juilliard. And on top of all this, I find myself thinking about Ben Wheeler's green-olive eyes at the most random moments, like, oh, say, right now.

My dad finally gives up. "The derivative of a constant times a function is the constant times the derivative of the function," he says. "Here, let me show you how this works." His pencil flies across the page, numbers filling up the empty white space. Soon he forgets I'm even in the same room with him. Numbers do that to him—he is more comfortable creating new software protocols or reconfiguring some computer program than he is talking and interacting with other, you know, human beings.

When I started school (i.e., kindergarten), my dad was so anxious for me to do well in math that he would make me learn ahead. It got a little out of hand. For example, I took pre-algebra in the seventh grade and got an A in it. But my dad bought an algebra I textbook and taught me from that book at home, while I had to keep up with my seventh-grade pre-algebra homework in school.

But he is from a different generation, from an era that taught "old math." Old math is all about the numbers. In my school they teach "new math," which emphasizes the relationships among those numbers.

For example, let's talk about sets and subsets. My

dad taught me that if you have a set called (A) and (A) is a subset of another subset {B}, then every element that is in (A) is also in {B}.

If you want to get really technical, you could say counting numbers (1, 2, 3 . . .) are a subset of whole numbers {0, 1, 2, 3 . . . }, and that would look like this:

(1, 2, 3) is a subset of {0, 1, 2, 3} = {0, (1, 2, 3)}

I know. It gets confusing.

But with the new math being taught at school, I'm learning about how to apply these cold numbers to real life. So here's another way of looking at sets and subsets.

Patti Yoon's Class Schedule:		Ben Wheeler's Class Schedule[9]:	
1st period:	Gym	1st period:	Gym
2nd period:	AP English	2nd period:	Senior English
3rd period:	AP Latin IV	3rd period:	Trigonometry
4th period:	AP calculus	4th period:	Band
Lunch		Lunch	
5th period:	AP physics	5th period:	Latin II
6th period:	AP psychology	6th period:	Biology
7th period:	AP economics	7th period:	Humanities

[9] I peeked at his schedule during homeroom when he wasn't looking.

This means Ben is a subset of me. As a result, the classes we share together are:

Homeroom
1st period Gym
Lunch

See? It's all about the relationship between numbers, not just the numbers themselves.

"Take a look at this." My dad's voice startles me. I sit up straight and try to look alert. He slides over his paper, now covered with numbers and symbols and graphs. "Once you determine the critical numbers . . ."

Stop thinking about Ben! I force myself to listen carefully as he explains the solution. Slowly it starts to make sense. "So these are the values of x that make the derivative of A equal zero," I say.

My dad smiles. "Good! You got it!"

"Yeah, after like an hour," I say, frowning.

"Don't be frustrated," he says. "Calculus is a very difficult subject. I had so much trouble with calculus that my parents had to save money so I could attend a *hagwon* in order to pass the college entrance exams."

"What's a *hagwon*?" My dad rarely talks about his life in Korea.

"A private school I had to attend after school," he says.

"You went to school twice?"

He shrugs as if that isn't a big deal. "Of course. After school ended, I then went to *hagwon* every day from two o'clock in the afternoon until ten at night. I also went to *hagwon* on Saturdays and Sundays. I studied every day for fourteen straight hours until exam day. And you know what exam day is. . . ."

"I know, I know," I say. I've only heard my parents mention Korea's exam day at least once a day, and how exam day makes the SATs feel like kindergarten recess.

As always, my dad decides to remind me one more time about how difficult and traumatic exam day was for him and my mom. "In Korea the only way you can go to college is to pass a very difficult exam," he says as I stare down at the carpet. "Parents will go to church or to a Buddhist temple on exam day to pray for their children. It's crucial for students to be accepted into the top Korean universities. That's the only way to get a job and have a career."

"Yeah, and you end up homeless if you fail," I say, trying to rush the conversation forward so we can get back to this calculus nightmare and finish it, because I still have another four hours of homework to do tonight.

"That's not funny," my dad says.

I look up from the carpet. He has this sad expression on his face. I've never seen him look so sad before. What did I say wrong? "I'm sorry," I say, not sure what else to say.

"If you fail the exam and don't go to college—" He is quiet for a moment. "That is very, very bad. The first time I took the exam, I failed. My mother wept when we received the scores. I was so ashamed."

What? I have never heard this part of the story before. I can't believe this is the first time my dad has admitted failing the exam to me. "What happened after that?" I ask.

"I had to take the exam again."

"Did you pass?"

"Yes. But the shame I brought upon my family is a burden I have to carry for the rest of my life."

Burden? *Shame?* It's just math! I had no idea

Koreans took education *that* seriously. No wonder my parents don't talk much about their lives in Korea to me. It's almost like a life-or-death situation. I always took it for granted that my dad graduated easily with honors from Seoul National University, which is often called the Harvard of Korea. I didn't know he had to study fourteen hours a day with a private tutor in order to get into college. Suddenly my life doesn't seem so awful. Okay, well, my life is still pretty lousy, but at least I don't have to deal with a *hagwon*. Although I guess you could say that right now Sunday-night math review in the kitchen with my dad is sort of like a *hagwon*. I feel bad for daydreaming about Ben, especially after learning about how hard my dad worked when he was my age. I bet he didn't daydream about *anything*. Shame is a good motivator.

"Let's get back to work." He points. "And here, the interval of 0, 8 . . ." There's this lightness in his voice as he continues to explain the solution to the problem. My dad is actually happy. But it's not the numbers that make him happy. It's the process, the discovery of a solution that makes him smile. For the first time, I wonder—did my dad pursue a career in computers because he was good at it or because math and numbers and computers made him happy? And is there a difference?

Even though my dad is helping me find the answer to this one question, there are now suddenly many more questions that I don't know the answers to.

Proof

Arma virumque cano, Troiae qui primus ab oris
Italiam, fato profugus, Laviniaque venit
litora, multum ille et terris iactatus et alto. . . .

So far I've figured out that *"Arma virumque cano"* translates to "Arms and the man I sing," but the rest is kind of hard. Something about a fugitive coming to the shores of Italy.

I raise my arms over my head and stretch. Thanks to Eric's harassment, I'm sitting in my usual lunch-hour spot—the last study carrel in the back corner of the library—doing my homework and listening to the

Mendelssohn Violin Concerto (this time the Itzhak Perlman recording) on my iPod.

In my AP Latin IV class, we're translating Virgil's *Aeneid*. Given how difficult this Latin assignment is, I figure I'll get my translations done every day at lunch. That way I'll have an extra hour every night to practice my violin or do another SAT practice test.

Someone sits down in the study carrel in front of me. After a few seconds, the sound of a tinny guitar blares. Someone's also listening to music on an iPod, but at a really, really loud volume. It's totally over-powering my Mendelssohn.

Great. First Eric, now this. There's no way I can concentrate with that annoying sound. I'm braver this time because the library is *my* turf. I'm not going to walk away. I stand up and lean over. There's a guy sitting in the next study carrel, his back facing me, his head bobbing up and down to the music blaring from his earbuds.

I take off my earbuds and tap his shoulder. "Excuse me, can you turn that down?" I snap.

He turns around. Oh great. Good move, Patti Yoon.

Ben removes his earbuds. "Hey Patti," he says, smiling. "What did you say?"

Suddenly I don't mind the tinny guitar sounds floating from the earbuds into the air. "Oh, I wanted to know what you were listening to," I say quickly.

"The Sex Pistols," he says.

"The what?"

"The Sex Pistols. 'Never Mind the Bollocks.' You've never heard of them?"

I briefly consider lying to him. But there's something in the tone of his voice that makes me realize he's not going to make fun of me if I admit my ignorance. I decide to be honest. "No."

"If you like The Clash, you'll really like these guys. Here, take a listen." He stands up and places his earbuds in my ears, the tips of his fingers brushing against my skin. I clutch the edge of my desk to keep from swaying, I am so giddy. This is the closest he's ever gotten to me. At the same time, a wall of sound surrounds me— a raucous guitar line crunching against a frenzied drumming, a singer with a British accent yowling about anarchy.

After all my years of music theory, I can immediately identify the three chords that this band is playing over and over without variation. The singer's out of tune, the bass guitar rushes the beat, and the guitar sounds distorted. It's too loud, too crude, and just plain awful. It's no Mendelssohn.

And yet I find myself drawn to this strange new music. There's a rage spilling through the notes that strikes a place deep inside me.

Ben smiles. His lips move as he speaks, but I can't hear him over the music.

"What?" I shout.

He fumbles for the iPod and turns it off. "Shhh," he whispers, looking around, grinning. "You'll get us kicked out."

I hand back the earbuds. "Sorry," I whisper. "What did you say?"

"I asked if you liked it."

I nod.

"Me too. I love this album. Everything on the radio is so fake. These guys are raw."

"Yeah, raw," I echo. At this point, Ben could say just about anything and I'd agree with him. There's a moment of silence. I don't want this conversation to end. "You know who's really raw?" I say.

"No, who?" He leans forward.

"Shostakovich." The name feels really out of place in our conversation, and I know I suddenly sound like a geek. But I force myself to continue talking. "He's a Russian composer. I think you'd like some of his string quartets—they're raw like this band."

His eyebrows draw together in puzzlement, as if I'm speaking Russian. Then he points to my copy of *The Aeneid*. "What class is that for?"

"Latin IV."

"Are you any good at translations?"

"Yes." I hesitate. "Well, not today. This is pretty hard stuff."

He reaches for his Latin II textbook and holds it up. "What about this?"

His textbook is open to a passage by Cicero. I recognize it immediately—Cicero's *"De Amicitia."* On Friendship.

"See, I can't figure out this part," he says, pointing to one paragraph that begins: *"Ut enim quisque sibi plurimum confidit et . . ."*

"That's my favorite passage," I say, immediately wincing at how nerdy I sound. But Ben doesn't laugh.

"Why?"

"Because . . ." My voice fades. This is the longest conversation we have ever had together. Why am I wasting it by talking about Latin? I rush along, trying to change the subject, wanting us to talk more about music and less about homework. "In this passage Cicero is saying that friendship is its own reward." I point to his iPod. "Can I hear that band again?"

But Ben doesn't answer my question. "You've translated this before?" He looks at me a little too eagerly. I recognize the look—it's the same look Maura once gave me last year when I helped her pass geometry. The warmth in my heart cools as I wonder if Ben has only been acting nice to me this whole time so I can do his Latin homework for him.

"Yes," I say, my voice no longer friendly. It's my polite voice, the one I use with Kyung Hee at church. My stomach hurts.

"You're the brainiac. Can you tell me if I did this right?" he asks, giving me his notebook.

To my surprise, Ben has already translated the entire passage, and quite eloquently.

"The more confident a man, the more he is strengthened by the wisdom that he needs no one. He decides that

his happiness depends on himself, and he excels in seeking out friendships."

"It's really good," I say, my heart and stomach lurching in confusion because it's turning out that Ben isn't being nice in order to get me to do his homework, because he already did it. He just wanted my opinion because he thinks I'm smart. He's just being . . . a nice guy.

I scribble down a few corrections, explaining to Ben how to fix the mistakes: "You could also translate this to say 'For the more confidence a man has in himself' and here, it's not 'he decides,' it's 'he judges.' And here, instead of 'he needs no one,' it's really, 'he stands in need of no one.'"

I hand back his notebook.

"Thanks," he says. "That's so nice of you. Well, I should stop bothering you."

You're not bothering me, I think. I glance at my watch—there's a few minutes left before the bell rings for fifth period. Before I can stop myself, I blurt out: "Do you know what *in vino veritas* means?" This was one of the first Latin phrases I learned in the ninth grade, and I always found it funny. But somehow, asking this out loud to a track team captain makes me sound like such a loser.

Ben shakes his head and waits. It's too late to back out. I take a deep breath and say, "It means, 'In wine there is truth.'"

To my relief, he smiles. "I like that," he says. I love how he speaks to me, his tone gentle and sweet.

And then he says something that nearly stops my heart. "Hey, who was that Russian guy you mentioned before? Shosta-something?"

"Shostakovich," I say quickly.

"Yeah. Can you burn me a CD of his stuff? I'd be interested to hear what he sounds like."

"Burn a CD," I repeat, in shock as I realize Ben actually listened to me when I was babbling earlier about Shostakovich.

"Yeah, a classical mix." He grins. "It'll be cool. I'll put together a CD for you, too, of some bands I think you'd really like."

Oh my God. I can't stand it. I think my heart is going to burst into confetti.

"There you are." Stephanie walks over. She ignores me completely. "You disappeared on me during lunch."

"Sorry," Ben says. "I had to get some homework done."

"Did you hear about the party?" she asks him. "Eric's parents are out of town Saturday. His older brother's getting three kegs."

Wait a second. Why is Stephanie interrupting us to talk about Eric's party? Why did she even leave the cafeteria to find Ben? Oh my God, are they *dating*?

"We can go after Saturday's track meet," she says. Her tone is casual, as if she and Ben always go to parties together.

"Sounds good," Ben says. His tone is casual, too, as if . . . *he could be her boyfriend.*

When I took honors geometry in the tenth grade, we had a whole unit on logic because mathematical proofs are basically deductive arguments. We learned all these formulas on valid arguments, such as Affirming the Consequent:

If P, then Q. *If Socrates is a man, then Socrates is mortal.*

Q. *Socrates is a man.*

Therefore P. *Therefore, Socrates is mortal.*

But in order for a proof to be logical, it also has to

be valid. In other words, you can't reverse the logic. Just because Socrates is mortal doesn't necessarily mean he is human. He could be a dog because dogs are mortal. It gets very complicated. The trick is to make sure that there is truth behind the argument.

If P, then Q. *If Stephanie and Ben are dating, Ben will drive Stephanie to Eric's party.*

Q. *Ben will drive Stephanie to Eric's party.*

Therefore P. *Therefore, Stephanie and Ben are dating.*

"How about I pick you up at four?" Ben asks Stephanie.

My heart sinks. I can't find a flaw in this proof. Ben and Stephanie *must* be dating.

"Sure," Stephanie says.

"Cool." Ben turns to me. "Patti, are you going too?"

What? Not only does Ben assume I actually go to parties, but that *I actually go to parties held at Eric's house.*

"Maybe," I say quickly, not sure how to answer him.

He smiles. "Got a packed social schedule, huh?" There it is, his dry wit and low-key tone. I feel like I've been included in Ben's private circle of friends. Okay, let's try this logic again:

If P, then Q. *If Ben likes me, he will ask if I am going to Eric's party.*

Q. *Ben asked if I was going to Eric's party.*

Therefore P. *Therefore, Ben likes me.*

Of course, as with the Socrates is mortal/human argument, there is a tiny flaw in this new proof. Just because Ben likes me doesn't mean he can't like Stephanie, too. In fact, there's no reason why he couldn't like Stephanie a bit more than me.

Stephanie's eyes narrow. She sniffs and looks away, completely dismissing my presence and my very existence.

Ben hands me his iPod. "Let's trade," he says. "You can borrow mine. Let me know what songs you like, and I'll download them for you."

The bell rings before I can say thank you. *If Ben likes me, he will trade iPods with me.* I smile like an idiot because I'm holding on to Ben's iPod. I keep smiling as Ben says good-bye. Stephanie links her arm through the crook of his elbow as if to remind me that he belongs to her as they walk away. I don't care. I put the iPod into my jacket pocket. For the rest of the day, I can feel its weight, resting against my side. For now, it's all the proof I need to convince myself that yes, I still have a chance with Ben.

Problems

"Too many problems / Oh why am I here. . . ."

I think I've listened to Ben's entire iPod at least ten times in a row now. I nearly knock my soda all over the Harvard application as I pretend to play the guitar along with the song "Problems" by the Sex Pistols. I wonder if I could ever make this kind of sound on my violin.

I'm grateful for this music—I don't know how I would have survived Friday night, sitting alone in my room, putting together a college application checklist of deadlines and dates.

It's weird, but the more I listen to this one song, the

angrier I get. I can't help but think about everything in my life that is driving me crazy right now: Eric "Ching Chong" Sanders, field hockey hell, SATs, trying to grasp the concept of transcendental functions in AP calc, memorizing the Mendelssohn, being assistant concertmaster of All-State, the Juilliard application hiding in my violin case, Stephanie and Ben at Eric's keg party tomorrow, Stephanie and Ben possibly dating.

I scroll back to the first song. The sounds of stomping feet fill my ears right before the drums, followed by a distorted guitar chord. He's playing a D major chord, which is usually such a bright, happy-sounding one, but somehow this bright chord sounds so menacing. "I don't want a holiday in the sun. . . ." the singer growls.

What is Ben doing tonight? I know he has a track meet tomorrow. Maybe he's staying in tonight too. I wonder if he's doing his homework or watching TV. I wonder if he is out on a date with Stephanie. I wonder if they're having fun and holding hands.

Why can't I stop thinking about him? It's very distracting. I could have already gotten some homework done tonight, or finished another SAT prep test.

Does Ben ever think of me?

Maybe he does. Maybe at some point over the weekend, Ben will stop thinking about Stephanie and Eric's party and about the track meet and finishing his Latin II homework and about everything else important in his life. And at that very moment, Ben will remember that we traded iPods and that we promised to make CDs of our favorite music for each other. For a few brief, glorious seconds he will be thinking only of me.

Monday Morning in Homeroom—
My CD for Ben Wheeler

Bartók String Quartet no. 1, op. 7
Performed by the Emerson String Quartet
Track 1—Movement 1, *Lento—attaca*
Track 2—Movement 2, *Poco a poco accelerando
all'Allegretto—Introduzione—Allegro
attaca*
Track 3—Movement 3, *Allegro vivace*

Shostakovich String Quartet no. 8 in C Minor
Performed by the Emerson String Quartet
Track 4—Movement 1, *Largo*
Track 5—Movement 2, *Allegro molto*
Track 6—Movement 3, *Allegretto*
Track 7—Movement 4, *Largo*
Track 8—Movement 5, *Largo*

Monday Morning in Homeroom—
Ben's CD for Me

Track 1—The Velvet Underground, "Rock and Roll"
Track 2—Violent Femmes, "Prove My Love"
Track 3—Sex Pistols, "Anarchy in the UK"
Track 4—Suicidal Tendencies, "Institutionalized"
Track 5—MC 5, "Kick Out the Jams"
Track 6—Buzzcocks, "Ever Fall in Love (With Someone You Shouldn't've)?"
Track 7—Iggy Pop and the Stooges, "Search and Destroy"
Track 8—The Clash, "White Riot"
Track 9—Black Flag, "Gimmie Gimmie Gimmie"
Track 10—Dead Kennedys, "Terminal Preppie"

Permanent Storage

I'm stumped. I'm hiding out in the library for lunch, and I don't know if I should start reading Jean-Paul Sartre's play *No Exit* for our next AP English assignment, take a practice SAT test, or read the next chapter of my AP econ textbook, "The Market Forces of Supply and Demand and Government Policies."

As I sit here, panicking because I'm not utilizing my spare time in a productive manner, someone taps me on the shoulder. I look up. To my surprise, it's Ben.

"We have to stop meeting like this," I say before I can stop myself. I can't help it—whenever I'm around

Ben, I start to babble and say stupid things that he seems to find funny.

To my relief, he still thinks I'm funny. He laughs.

Oh, who cares about market forces and government policy? I lean back in my chair, trying to look nonchalant, like I'm used to hanging out with Ben in the back of the library.

"Thanks for the CD," he says. "I can't wait to listen to it."

"You're welcome," I say. "Thanks for mine, too." Please, please don't walk away. I think frantically, looking for something else to say, anything to keep him here with me. But for someone who's taking six AP courses, I've got nothing. Absolutely nothing to say because I'm staring into his green-olive eyes and have turned into a complete moron. He is so cute *I can't stand it.*

"I actually stopped by because I wanted to ask you something," he says.

Oh my God!

"You know I play guitar, right?" he continues.

"Yeah," I say, not sure where this is headed.

"I used to be in a band in Michigan. I wrote some

new songs, and I thought a violin would be cool to add in. You interested?"

Can't. Speak. Must. Nod. Head.

"Patti?"

Say something! "Sure. Yeah. Okay. Uh-huh. Of course. I'd love to. . . ." *You can stop talking now, Patti!* I shut up. I'm still pleased, however, with how casual I sound, as if I always get asked by cute guys to play my violin on some new songs they've just written.

"Cool. I was thinking, maybe, you wanna come over this Saturday?"

"Okay," I say, even though I haven't asked my parents for permission yet because I know there's no way they would let me do this. It would distract me from my studies, and I would spend time with some strange boy. But I still say yes because I am not going to ruin this moment.

"Cool." He pulls a pen from his backpack and takes my right hand with his left. His fingers curl against the back of my hand as he writes his address down with his right hand, the ink smeared across my skin but still legible. *Ben—123 Country Club Road.*

"Okay, I'll leave you alone." He nods at my books.

"You look busy, brainiac." He lets go of my hand and walks off.

When I took AP honors biology in tenth grade, we learned about how memory works and how the capacity for long-term memory is endless, whether you memorized the information five minutes ago or five years ago. But when it came to remembering important events in your life, those memories would be sent to the part of the brain called the hippocampus. After time, those memories would be transferred to the neocortex for permanent storage.

So if you keep thinking about a special person or event long enough, it will be impossible to erase that memory. You'll be stuck with the memory for the rest of your life. I guess you have to be careful about what you think is important in your life.

I trace the letters of *Ben—123 Country Club Road* over and over on my palm, trying as hard as I can to transfer this memory to my permanent storage.

My Mom's Spam Recipe #2—
Spicy Spam Ramen Noodles

Ingredients:
1 can of Spam
1 jar of kimchi
1 package of instant ramen noodles
1 egg
Green onions
Bottle of *kochu jang*

Directions:
1. Dice Spam into 1-inch cubes and fry.
2. Boil water in a separate pan. Once the water boils, dump in a package of instant ramen noodles. Don't forget to open that little aluminum package of dry spice mix and stir it in.
3. Dump fried Spam cubes into the noodles.
4. Stir in all the kimchi and *kochu jang* sauce you want. (Note: Again, I'm assuming you know where to buy *kochu jang*. If you don't, try to

find the nearest Korean church in your town and sneak into their kitchen and borrow the giant bottle of *kochu jang* from the Korean church kitchen's refrigerator. Don't forget to return it afterward, because "Thou Shalt Not Steal" is the eighth commandment.)

5. Pour everything into a giant bowl.
6. Now crack an egg and drop it into the bowl. The heat from the noodles and boiled broth will cook the egg.
7. Or poach the egg first if you're scared of raw eggs and things like salmonella bacteria (you'll realize you have salmonellosis within 6 to 72 hours after eating an infected raw egg—come to think of it, maybe it's a bad idea to discuss salmonella poisoning while describing how to make another one of my mom's Spam dishes . . .).
8. Dice a couple stalks of green onions and garnish the top.
9. Enjoy!

My mom's spicy Spam ramen noodles has become a late-night Friday study-break snack. We sit in the kitchen with our steaming bowls of Spam ramen, slurping away. I break the egg and mix the yolk with the noodles. I'm starving after having taken three SAT practice tests in a row.

"Can I have more kimchi?" I ask. My mom slides the jar over. I dump some into the bowl.

"What were your scores on the practice tests?" my mom asks.

"700 Math, 700 Verbal, 700 Writing."

"That's not good enough," she says.

"I know, but at least I didn't score below a 700 on any section," I say.

My mom smiles. "That's an improvement."

We eat in silence. I take a deep breath. "Mom, I have to ask you something."

"What is it?"

"There's this friend of mine at school, this friend is a musician, and this friend wrote some songs on guitar and wants me to play violin on these songs, this friend wants me to go over to his house to rehearse and . . ." *Patti!* You messed up and used a pronoun! *Augh!*

"*His* house?"

138

My mom is a hawk. She misses nothing. I nod, miserable.

"No," she says. "You don't have time to waste playing music with some boy from your school. He'll have to find someone else."

Her tone is firm. I know there's no way to convince her otherwise. My stomach hurts. I look down at my spicy Spam ramen noodles. They're starting to congeal along the sides of the bowl.

You know, I think I'm getting a little tired of all this Spam.

A Helpful SAT Tip

Sometimes the method of "backsolving," or making an educated guess, is the only way to answer a math question, especially when it's a complicated word problem with algebraic equations as your only choices.[10]

Student A's mom won't let her go to Ben Wheeler's house on Saturday after orchestra rehearsal at the University of Hartford.

Student A decides to lie to her parents. She says she signed up for another SAT boot camp class also being held on campus after rehearsal and that's why she won't be home until six o'clock. The truth is that Student B is the only one who signed up for SAT boot camp.

Student B has his driver's license and often

---

[10]In other words, take a wild guess when you know you're screwed and have no idea what the answer is.

140

carpools with Student A because Student A's parents won't let her drive by herself even though she scored a perfect 100% on both her written and driving tests at the Connecticut DMV last year. (They're afraid she might get into a minor car accident, thus ruining her chances of getting into HYP.)

The SAT boot camp class starts 25 minutes after orchestra rehearsal ends. Ben's house is 17.4 miles away from the campus. Student B also obeys the 35-mile-per-hour speed limit on Bloomfield Ave.

Which of the following equations could be used to find the exact miles per hour Student B has to drive at in order to drop Student A off at Ben Wheeler's house with enough time left to drive back to his SAT boot camp class before anyone notices?

A) $\dfrac{x}{60} = \dfrac{34.8}{25}$

B) $25x = 34.8y + 60$

C) $\dfrac{x}{34.8} = \dfrac{25}{60}$

D) $\dfrac{x}{60} = \dfrac{25}{34.8}$

E) A and B

F) None of the above

College Essay Question No.3

3. Evaluate a significant ethical or moral dilemma
   you have faced and its impact on you.

"Samuel, you have to go faster," I say. "Like, 83.52 miles faster."

"But the speed limit's thirty-five miles per hour," Samuel says. He grips the wheel, his knuckles white, as we crawl along Bloomfield Avenue.

I lean back and sigh. I'd better stop bugging Samuel—otherwise he might change his mind. I'm lucky he even agreed to drive me at all. It's 3:03 on a Saturday afternoon, and we're now 14.5 miles away

142

from Ben Wheeler's house. There's no way Samuel's going to make it back to class in time if he keeps going at the 35-mph speed limit.

"Pull over," I say.

"What?"

"Pull over! Let's switch! I'll drive!"

"Patti, you're not listed on my dad's car insurance. I could get in big trouble."

"Sam, you'll get us both into bigger trouble if we don't get to Ben's house by 3:13. How are you going to make it back in time for SAT boot camp?"

"That's it. We're going back. I never should've let you talk me into this. I'm gonna get a demerit."

He switches on the blinker and prepares to turn around. I think fast. Very fast. Hang on. Wait a minute. Why is Samuel Kwon, certified math genius, taking SAT boot camp again? He took the SAT in June with me and never told me his score.

I grab his book bag from the backseat. I pull out his SAT boot camp folder and skim through it and . . . wow. It's even worse than I had thought. I can't help but gasp.

"Samuel Kwon, you got a 550 on the writing test?"

"Give me that!" He lunges for the folder, and the car kind of lunges, too, and we almost run off the road.

"Watch out!" I yell.

Samuel grabs the steering wheel and manages to avoid hitting three cars while drifting two lanes over to the left.

"I'll tell everyone at church on Sunday," I threaten.

Samuel doesn't say a word. He presses his foot down on the accelerator. I lean back, satisfied, as the needle on the speedometer slowly swings up to 45 miles per hour and keeps steadily climbing.

Jamming

It's a little embarrassing at first. Here I am, Greater Hartford Youth Orchestra concertmaster *and* Connecticut All-State Orchestra assistant concertmaster, and I can play only simple scales above Ben's chords. I'm so distracted by this that I forget how cute Ben is, because all I can think of is What note should I play next?

For the past hour we've been "jamming" in Ben's room, me on violin and Ben on his acoustic guitar. I quickly learned that "jamming" meant Ben would play a few chords and then wait for me to play something on top of those chords, like a melody. Which was much harder than I thought it would be—I'm used to reading music, not making it up by ear on the spot. Then his mom kept popping in, asking if we wanted something to eat, and I was distracted because I kept staring at her, trying to see the resemblance between Ben and his mom. (He has her green-olive eyes and wavy brown hair, but she's really short, so I think his dad must be tall.)

Right now Ben is playing the same three chords over and over, but so far the only thing I've been able to do all afternoon is match the top note of each chord so we're at least in the same key.

But I'm getting bored. All I'm playing are long whole notes. I don't want Ben to think I'm some beginner violinist who can play only slow notes, so I quickly do a glissando followed by a couple of octave slides and a fancy spiccato-style bowing to show off my skills.

He stops playing. "I liked what you did earlier," he says.

"You mean this?" I play the simple scale again.

"Yeah," he says. "Patti, I know you're a really advanced musician. But in rock music, less is more, you know? It's all about finding a cool riff and repeating it.

Throw out all your classical training and all that music theory. Don't think, just play."

I reach for a pencil on his desk. "Wait. Let me write down what I just played."

He shakes his head. "No need to write it down."

"But I won't remember exactly what I just did."

"That's okay—you'll come up with something else." He sounds so confident in my jamming abilities.

Suddenly playing music with Ben isn't fun anymore. There's too much pressure now. "But—"

He laughs. "Don't freak out, Patti. I don't care if you make mistakes. The notes don't matter, just the energy. Does that make sense?"

"I just like everything to be perfect."

"Perfect Patti," he says, his eyes twinkling. "Don't think, just play."

Although I'm a more technically advanced musician than Ben, he definitely plays circles around me when it comes to improvising music off the top of his head. I listen as he plays the same simple scale back and then adds a few embellishments here and there to spice up the tune. But the few embellishments don't distract from the main melody. His fingers dash up and down the guitar frets. I notice how long and lean his fingers are, callused flat at the fingertips. His hair falls over, hiding half his face, as he continues to jam, swept up in the music.

I close my eyes and really listen to what he's playing. I ignore the part of my brain already analyzing the chord progressions and figuring out the harmonies. *Don't think, just play.*

I raise my violin and join in, playing a long, sustained note that hovers just above Ben's melody. A rhythm builds between us, and without planning it, I take over the chords and Ben plays the melody, improvising a new variation. The pressure not to make any mistakes disappears. I love this! I want to jam forever. This is so much fun.

Ben looks up and signals that we should wrap this up. I follow his lead, and we end on the same note together. He grins. "That was cool."

I smile back. "We were in the zone."

"The zone?"

"It's hard to explain," I say. "It's like, when I play the violin, I get into the zone and the world outside disappears. All I can hear is the music, and all I can feel is this." I hold up my violin and bow.

He nods. "Sounds like when I run. I get into this zone where all I can see are my feet and the ground."

I point to all the trophies and certificates on his bookshelf. "You're really good at running. What do you like better—track or cross-country?"

"I used to like both. But now running's become this thing I have to do. My dad's always on my back about leading the pack more at meets. Says I have to push myself harder."

He plays a chord on the guitar. "But I'm getting more into music. I might not do track in the spring. My dad'll be pissed."

"But you can't quit," I say. "Look at all these state championship trophies. It's your hook for college."

He laughs. "My what?"

"You know, a hook. Something that sets you apart from the others."

"Like your violin?"

I nod.

"But you *like* to play the violin. It's not just a hook for you. You're applying to music schools, right?"

In a rush, I hear my parents' voices in my head. *HARVARDYALEPRINCETON.* I shake my head.

"Really? So where do you want to go?"

"I'm applying to HarvardYalePrinceton," I say.

"Why?" He genuinely sounds surprised. "You're such a great musician. Why give that up?"

First Mr. Mishkind, now Ben. I haven't even looked at the Juilliard application Mr. Mishkind gave me—it's still hidden away in my violin case. But as Ben asks me these questions I can't answer, I look at the violin nestled in my arms and feel sad again. I think about how happy I feel when I play the Mendelssohn, how happy I just felt jamming with Ben, and how every single concert and recital I've done since kindergarten has made me that happy. Again I'm forced to imagine life after graduation without any music. And it feels empty.

"I don't want to give up music," I finally say. "But it's hard to explain."

He nods. "It's not. I know what you're going to say. You can't make a living as a musician. I get that all the time from my parents. Which is why I'll probably major in accounting. But you're so talented, you actually could make a living, a really good one, as a musician."

"My violin teacher told me to apply to Juilliard," I say.

"See?" He looks so triumphant.

"But I can't."

"Why not?"

"It's not part of the plan."

"Whose plan? Yours? Or your parents'?"

"It's my plan," I say, my shoulders stiffening. I feel a little defensive now—why is he giving me such a hard time? It's none of his business what I do in the future. And it *is* my plan.

He looks puzzled. "So your plan is to do whatever your parents want, right?"

"We want the same things," I say. But Ben doesn't look convinced. You know, maybe he does have a point. My parents want me to get into HYP so they can brag about it to their friends in church and because it will make them proud. Why do I want HYP? I want to be the best, I want to get into HYP, I want to get out of Woodward and away from idiots like Eric Sanders and Stephanie Thomas. This is the only way I know how.

"You should choose to do something you like, something that makes you happy," he says. My stomach flutters—he looks so handsome, the way he's staring at me intensely, not bothering to brush the hair out of his eyes. "What do you like to do? What makes you happy?"

Being with you, I think. "You're right," I finally say. "I love playing the violin. Music makes me happy. But it's not about what I want or what makes me happy. It's about doing what's right."

"How do you know that applying to music school is wrong?"

"This might sound weird, but getting straight As makes me happy too," I say. I can't believe how easy it is to be honest like this, how easy it is to talk with Ben Wheeler as if we have known each other our whole lives. "I wouldn't have worked this hard if I didn't like to learn new things. Getting into Harvard, Yale, and Princeton would make me really happy."

"Of course," he says. "Nothing but the best for Patti Yoon."

There it is again—that gentle teasing tone in his voice. I glance at him, and suddenly everything goes hazy and my vision blurs. It's like I'm staring down a dark tunnel, and his voice is my only guide. I realize in this moment that I could listen to his voice forever.

Ben puts away his guitar. "I have a track meet next

Saturday, but you wanna do this again in a couple of weeks?" he asks.

AAAAIEEEEE!!!!! "Sure, sounds good," I say casually as I wipe the rosin dust from my violin with a soft cloth.

"Cool." He shuts the guitar case.

I put away my violin and pull out my cell phone, about to call Samuel to see if he can pick me up now, when Ben asks, "Do you need a ride home?"

Do you need a ride home? The six most beautiful words I have ever heard. "Yes," I say calmly, trying to keep my voice from shaking.

"Let's go," he says.

I follow Ben to the garage. He holds out his hand. I give him my violin case, and he places it in the trunk of his car.

So what if Ben and Stephanie might be dating. They might not be, too! It can't hurt to pretend I'm his girlfriend. After all, it's not every day that someone who looks like Ben Wheeler offers to drive me home on a Saturday afternoon. When he walks over to the passenger door and unlocks it for me, I say, "Thanks," and smile my best flirtatious smile and bravely rest my hand on his arm for a millisecond before chickening out and letting go.

We drive to my house. The road dips and then rises again, the poplar and sycamore trees speeding past us in a hazy blur. I open the window and stick my head out, the wind crisp and cold against my face. The late-afternoon sun sparkles. I take a long, deep breath and look up into the blue, blue sky. It is so clear today.

Another Helpful SAT Tip

Memorize these three easy steps and the sentence completion portion of the SAT test will be a breeze.

1. Search for clue words in the sentence.
2. Predict the answer.
3. Compare/contrast your prediction against the answer choices.

Patti's _____ decisions as a volleyball player during Friday's gym class led to her burgeoning reputation as a/an _____ student athlete.

A) quick . . . capricious
B) equitable . . . wise
C) perceptive . . . adroit
D) incongruous . . . atrocious
E) None of the above

It was a bad scene. You don't want to know the answer.

Body Wave Perm

I can't believe I'm doing this. It's Friday night, and I'm standing in front of the bathroom sink, my scalp aching from the thirty-seven tight corkscrew rollers wrapped in my hair.

My mom is a body wave perm fanatic. She herself has one. I've seen pictures of her from the eighties, an era she still clings to with passionate fervor. Every year she begs me to try a perm, because she's convinced it will transform me from geek to gorgeous. Every year I refuse, because there's no way I can look as pretty as her. My mom is so pretty that people sometimes mistake her for my sister. She has thick black hair that curls

156

perfectly against her shoulders, good eyes, high cheek-bones, and a slim figure even though she never diets or exercises much.

Tomorrow I have another rehearsal with Ben. I was in the bathroom earlier tonight, using my mom's curling iron, trying to make my hair look more like Stephanie's with all her pretty layers, when my mom entered and suggested doing a home perm instead. "That way you wake up every day with curls and you don't have to waste time with the curling iron," she said. At the time it sounded like a good idea.

Now I'm wondering if this was such a wise decision. I've spent the past two hours sitting in the bathroom, waiting for the curling lotion to set my hair. Now it's time for the neutralizer solution. Okay, anything named The Neutralizer scares me.

My mom rips open three foil packages and mixes the liquids together into a small plastic bottle with a cap tip. It's like she's my lab partner in AP chem. She shakes up the bottle. "The neutralizer will make your curls last for many months," she says, holding the bottle over my head. It's too late for me to back out. She squeezes. The thick, viscous liquid mixture of chemicals oozes and coats my scalp with an icy sensation. The chemicals stink, all pungent and spicy, kind of like hot tar.

My mom carefully ties a cotton strip around my face. "This is to protect your skin," she says. A warning bell goes off in my brain—all that stands in the way of my skin and The Neutralizer is a delicate swatch of cheap cotton?

"It might leak," I say.

"Relax," my mom says. "You'll be fine." She squeezes the bottle empty and examines me. "Don't move. Sit here." She puts down the toilet lid and points to it. "I'll bring you a magazine."

I read the instructions on the back of the body perm wave box. *Place a small sample of the neutralizer chemical solution on the back of your hand to test for any allergic reaction,"* it reads. *"Let the solution sit for no more than 20 minutes. Any longer will lead to potential side effects—skin rash, breakage, a burning sensation.*

The Neutralizer leaks past the fragile, useless cotton barrier wrapped around my face and drips along the curve of my right ear.

I look around for a towel. Why is my ear feeling so

hot all of sudden? Did someone turn on the heat? Is it me, or is that burning flesh I smell? And then . . .

"Mom!"

"Coming," she shouts from down the hall. "Do you want the Barron's SAT test guide or the *Princeton Review*? How about some vocabulary flash cards?"

Vocabulary flash cards? How can my mom think about vocabulary flash cards when my *ear is burning off*! "Mom!" I scream. "Ear! Burns! Hurts!"

She appears in the doorway, clutching a handful of SAT test guides and a pack of vocabulary flash cards. "There's no redness," she says. "Don't worry. I use this brand all the time. It's not burning." She checks her watch. "Study these. I'll be back in twenty minutes."

At this point, I decide maybe I don't need my right ear. I can't feel anything in that area anymore. Everything's numb.

I spend the next twenty minutes testing myself with the vocab flash cards, starting with *Splenetic* (adj.): *Extremely bad-tempered or spiteful.* When the timer rings, my mom returns. She leans me carefully over the bathroom sink and removes the curlers. She rinses the rest of the neutralizer out of my hair. My head feels light, my hair bouncy. I'm eager to see what I look like—maybe this body wave perm's not such a bad idea.

"Oh no." She starts speaking in Korean.

"What?" I straighten up and look into the mirror.

I'm wearing a poodle on my head. I look sixty years old, my face framed by a mass of tight grandma curls. *"This is not a body wave perm,"* I wail. "This is a curly hair perm!"

My mom looks at the box. She waves it in my face. "No, it says here 'Body Wave Perm.'" She frowns. "I don't know why it looks like this." She pulls a ringlet straight and lets go. It bounces back. "Your hair's different from mine."

"I know," I shout.

My mom holds my chin in her hand and turns my face to the side. She gasps.

Okay, the thing with the gasping? Not a good sign.

"What?" I ask, looking in the mirror. The top of my right ear is bright red.

For the next ten minutes, my mom turns our bathroom into a triage center, bandaging up my burned ear.

"There," she says, her voice surprisingly gentle. She combs my new curls with her fingers and secures them with two hairpins. She turns me toward the mirror again. Although the tight curls still remind me of a poodle, at least now they're not framing my face like a halo. I look a little better, but there's no getting around how much of a huge mistake this was.

As I stare at myself in the mirror, I notice how this curly perm not only makes my chubby face even chubbier, it makes my nose even flatter. I imagine Stephanie and her thick, wavy blond hair and rosebud lips, and I realize there's no way Ben Wheeler would ever choose someone like me over her. I blink, my vision blurring.

"What's wrong? Does your ear still hurt?" For the first time in a long time, her voice isn't shrill. *"Ne gui ya un ah gi,"* she says. My dear baby.

I wipe my eyes. She hasn't called me that since I was a kid.

"Don't worry," she says, inspecting my ear again. "The medicine will work soon, and your ear will heal."

I'm about to tell her I'm not crying about my ear, but there's something in her eyes that stops me. She tugs at a curl and it bounces up and down.

"I like these curls now. I was a little surprised at first, but now I think they look cute."

161

I look at our reflection in the mirror and want to laugh. Me, with my poodle perm and flat nose and pudgy cheeks, next to my mom, with her graceful cheekbones, swan neck, and deep-set eyes. My mom is not only beautiful, she's also smart. Her beauty will never fade.

"Smile, Patti," she says. She smiles, and I notice thin wrinkles at the corners of her eyes and lips. "I want you to be happy." I see hope in her eyes, and I realize she truly does think I look nice with this awful poodle perm on my head. *I want you to be happy.*

"See?" My mom cups her hand under my chin and points to our reflection. "You look beautiful. Don't you think you look beautiful?"

I want you to be happy.

I take a deep breath and smile and say yes.

Top Ten Famous Female A-Tier Prodigy Violinists
Who Would Never Have Made That Stupid,
Embarrassing Memory Slip in the Mendelssohn
Like You Did During Today's Orchestra Rehearsal

1. Midori (made the front page of *The New York Times* at age fourteen)

2. Leila Josefowicz (debuted at Carnegie Hall when she was seventeen)

3. Esther Kim (accepted into Juilliard at ten)

4. Hilary Hahn (went to Curtis Institute, Juilliard's rival, at ten, won a Grammy later)

5. Anne-Sophie Mutter (was in the eighth grade when she recorded her first album)

6. Vanessa Mae (recorded her first album at ten, rebelled, and appeared in a wet T-shirt and nothing else on her second album when she was seventeen)

7. Rachel Barton (played with the Chicago Symphony at age ten)

8. Bin Huang (accepted into the Beijing

Conservatory at nine, later won the renowned
Paganini Competition)

9. Kyung-Wha Chung (was twelve when she
   entered Juilliard)
10. Sarah Chang (oh, we already know all about
    Sarah Chang!)

The Bridge

Not a G sharp!

Ben Wheeler just modulated to the key of D major. I'm still playing a G sharp from the previous key. The note clashes with what he's playing. He makes a face and stops.

"I thought you didn't care about wrong notes," I say, trying not to blush.

"Yeah, but not *that* wrong," he says. But he's smiling, so I know he's just kidding.

This is the fourth time I've been over to Ben's house after rehearsal for a jam session, thanks to Samuel's race-car driving skills. I've definitely gotten better at improvising—the more we jam, the easier it is to think quickly and come up with melodies and harmonies to match the guitar riffs Ben creates on the spot.

"Let's do the A section again before the prechorus and the bridge."

Huh? I always thought classical music was more sophisticated than rock music, but it turns out rock has its own set of weird terms and formal structures that are equally complicated and challenging, and— Ben puts his guitar back on the stand. "Earth to Patti!"

"I'm sorry," I say, looking away, my face red with embarrassment. "What's the bridge?"

"The bridge is the section that connects the parts of the song together," he explains. "Like a transition— Hey, what's that?" He points.

To my horror, he's pointing to the awful burn on my right ear from the Body Wave Perm Incident. My poodle-curly permed hair is pulled back in a frizzy ponytail. He reaches over and playfully tugs my ponytail.

I freeze. He examines the burn on my ear, his face so close to mine that his breath brushes against my skin. He smells faintly of toothpaste and detergent.

"How did this happen?" he asks.

I want to die, this is so embarrassing. I already came up with an elaborate story last night before I went to bed, but now I can't remember it, something stupid about trying out a new shampoo but not reading the ingredients label.

"It's nothing," I finally say.

Ben smiles, and once again, I swoon. For some reason I feel really comfortable around Ben. I can tell him anything and he won't laugh. "It's an allergic reaction," I say. "My mom gave me a home perm last night, and the solution burned my ear. I look so stupid."

"No, you don't," he says. "You look cute with those curls." He picks up his guitar and checks the tuning. "Okay, let's do the A part one more time before the bridge." He strums the opening chord.

But I'm not paying attention because now all I can think of is *Ben Wheeler thinks I LOOK CUTE!*

Ben stops playing. "Seriously, Patti, is everything okay? You've been pretty distracted all afternoon."

Of course I'm distracted! I want to shout at him. I'm distracted because you are wearing those beautiful faded jeans and the sleeves of your shirt are rolled up so when you grip the neck of your guitar these little veins pulse just beneath the skin on your wrist. Your hair is growing long again and it's covering your eyes when you play and you look so much like Simon Taylor from Jet Pack that it's killing me. It kills me how handsome you are and I wish you would kiss me and I can't believe I'm just sitting here *not doing anything about it.*

"I'm just stressed," I say casually. "You know, midterms, SATs, the usual."

"But you're always stressed about that stuff," he says. "Something else is bugging you."

How does he do it? How can Ben know me so well after only a few months? He knows me better than my parents, and I've been with them my whole life.

"I know what you're thinking about," he continues. My heart stops beating. I look away, embarrassed. Is my crush that obvious?

"Juilliard, right? You're thinking about applying now."

"I don't know," I say, relieved that Ben has no clue about how I really feel. "My parents wouldn't approve."

"But it's the best music school in the country. Aren't your parents all about being the best?"

"Yeah, but being a musician is really risky."

"Everything's risky."

"That's easy for you to say. You're not the one applying to Juilliard."

He grins. "You're scared of rejection." Oh, if only he knew the irony of that statement!

He leans forward. When he speaks, his breath brushes against my curls. It's very distracting. "Don't tell them," he says.

"What?"

"It can't hurt, right? Look, if Juilliard accepts you, your parents will be so proud that they won't care that you secretly applied. And if you're good enough to get into Juilliard, then becoming a musician may not be as risky as they think it is."

I have to admit it's very tempting. Logically Ben's argument makes perfect sense. "Well, I am performing the Mendelssohn concerto with my youth orchestra," I say. "That's one of the pieces required. I'd have to record that plus a couple other pieces. If they like my recording, then they'll ask me to show up for a live audition at the school."

"If you apply, they'll definitely ask you back for the live auditions." He sounds certain.

But I'm not so sure. "I'll think about it," I say.

"When's your orchestra concert?" he asks.

"November," I say.

"Can I come?" he asks. "I'd love to hear you play."

What? Did Ben Wheeler just ask if he could attend my youth orchestra concert?

"I have a digital recorder," he continues. "I could record it in case you change your mind about Juilliard." He points to his computer. "I also have a cool music recording software program. You could play right here in my room, and I can make it sound like you're playing in a concert hall. It's pretty neat."

I'm stunned. Why is he being so nice? No one's ever been this nice to me.

He smiles. "You're so lucky, you know that?"

Now I'm really confused and don't know what to say.

"You have nothing to worry about," he continues. "You're going to get into the best colleges, Miss HarvardYalePrinceton. You get to write your own ticket."

The question *Ben, are you crazy?!* pops into my head, but fortunately I have the good sense not to say that out loud. But he's got to be kidding—me having nothing to worry about? "Ben, that's really nice of you," I begin, "but I'm nothing compared to—"

"You, nothing?" He shakes his head. "I could never do what you do, all those AP classes, your activities, your music . . . Patti, you're amazing."

Ben, completely unaware of the seismic effect those three words, *Patti, you're amazing*, is having on me at this very moment, picks up his guitar. "Let's try that bridge again."

This time I don't play any wrong notes. As we near the end of the song, I finally understand, with brilliant clarity, why my heart stops every time I see Ben, why he takes my breath away, and why my stomach hurts in a good way every time he smiles at me.

It's because I don't have to prove myself to Ben by having straight As or scoring a 2300 on the SATs. Ben doesn't care about any of that. He likes me for me. I wonder if that's enough.

Top Ten Ways How Not to Be a P.K.D. (Perfect Korean Daughter)

1. You need an extension on your AP English paper, and you've never asked for a deadline extension before in your entire life.
2. You don't study enough for your AP calc test and receive your first B plus grade ever.
3. You forget to write up a list of items for the Lock-In scavenger hunt and receive a stern lecture on responsibility from Kyung Hee. In both English and Korean.
4. Instead of translating Virgil's *Aeneid* you spend two hours talking on the phone with Susan about how cute Ben is.
5. You read the latest tour blog from Jet Pack's official website and then anonymously post several opinions on their message board instead of taking another SAT practice math test.
6. You practice your jamming skills instead of

working on the cadenza to the Mendelssohn and practicing your All-State music.

7. You keep sneaking over to Ben's house to play music without your parents' knowledge and despite Samuel Kwon's protests.

8. During gym you hit the volleyball so far in the wrong direction that it breaks a window. Coach Turner has a hard time trying to find the positive side to this.

9. You disappoint Mr. Mishkind because you're still having problems memorizing the Mendelssohn.

10. You secretly start practicing the Paganini and Bach required for the Juilliard application CD.

No Exit

Today isn't your regular Friday. Today is Halloween. Everyone in school is dressed in costume. There's your usual assortment of monsters and vampires, plus some outrageous costumes including Eric dressed as a carton of milk with the word *missing* underneath his face. His friends are dressed as football zombies, which to me doesn't really seem like that much of a stretch. The only costume I like is Susan's—this year she's dressed as an elf queen.

I'm rummaging through my locker, looking for my copy of Sartre's *No Exit* for AP English, when Erin and Maura squeal.

Curious, I turn around. To my horror, Stephanie is taking really tiny steps as she scurries down the hallway dressed in a Japanese kimono, her face powdered white, her lips cherry red, and her blond hair hidden underneath an elaborate black wig. She waves a fan daintily in the air and bows to everyone she passes in the hall. When she passes by Eric the Missing Milk Carton Kid and his zombie friends, she flutters her eyelashes and says, "Sayonara."

Eric laughs. "Hey, my little China doll."

I want to scream, *"Geishas are Japanese, not Chinese, you moron."* Instead I'm rendered speechless when Stephanie flutters her eyelashes and says, "Me speakah no Engrish."

Are you kidding me?! I can't breathe. I wonder if she would have dressed up like this if I weren't the only Asian in my school, if there were two of me, or three, or four, or twenty, or a hundred.

As Geisha Stephanie shuffles up and down the hallway, to the hoots and whistles and cheers of the other students, I think about how my AP English test today is on Jean-Paul Sartre and existentialism: our futile desire to make rational decisions in an irrational world. I'd say that pretty much sums up my life here at Woodward High.

I flash to a line near the end of *No Exit*: "Hell is other people"! Tell me about it.

I slam my locker shut and whirl around . . . and bump straight into Stephanie. Her kimono is so tight that she loses her balance. I grab her arm to keep her from falling. She twists away from me.

"Watch it!" she snaps.

Hey, how about thank you? I lose it. "No," I snap back, raising my voice. "*You* watch it." I push past her and storm down the hall.

The murmurs swell as I head to my English class. "Did you hear what Chicken Patti said?" "What's her problem?" "She should get over herself."

But I couldn't care less about what Stephanie and everyone else thinks. I straighten my shoulders and hold my head high. You know what? My parents were right. I should be studying as hard as I can, I should be taking a billion SAT practice tests and score a 2300 or more. I'm going to study even harder, I will ace the SATs, and I will get accepted into every school I apply to. Because hell is other people at this school, and Ben Wheeler or no Ben Wheeler, I need to get the hell out of here.

87.5%

It's been two weeks since the Halloween Incident, and you know what? I finally scored a total of 2300 on my SAT practice tests!

Ironically, I have Stephanie to thank. After the Halloween/Stephanie-in-a-Geisha-Girl-Costume Incident, I barely said hello to my parents when I came home from school. Instead, I rushed up to my room. My mom followed me, and to her surprise I had already pulled out the SAT practice test book. She shut the door silently and left me alone in peace.

I've taken a practice SAT test every night since Halloween. The first night I scored a total of 2050. The next night a 2100. By the end of the first week I had made it to 2200.

Tonight, I did three SAT tests in a row. I blackened the circles next to the questions so deeply that the lead of my number 2 pencil kept chipping off. Total score? 2300.

If I can score at least a 2300 or higher every weekend on these practice tests, then I know I will score at least a 2300 on the real test in January.

How can I be so certain of this? It's your basic probability fraction:

$$\frac{\text{Number of favorable outcomes}}{\text{Total number of possible outcomes}}$$

Let's say I take the SAT practice test every weekend until January. That's eight tests. Let's say out of those eight tests, I score a 2300 or higher on at least seven of them.

That's ⅞.

So the probability of me scoring a 2300 or higher where all outcomes are equally likely is ⅞, or 87.5 percent. I'd say those are pretty good odds.

Factor in the combustible variable that I'm still really, really angry with Stephanie and everyone at my school, and the odds rise to at least 97.5 percent. Who knew anger would work so well? Think of all the money my parents could have saved on SAT boot camp!

Top Ten Reasons Why You're Afraid Your Youth Orchestra Will Fall Apart Performing the Mendelssohn Concerto

1. The trombone section flirts too much with the girls in the viola section.
2. The girls in the viola section wear too much makeup to rehearsal and are always reapplying their foundation during the rests in the music.
3. Our first oboist's reeds keep breaking, so she is always interrupting rehearsal to carve out a new one.
4. Susan, our first bassoonist, had her wisdom teeth removed last week, so she's having trouble playing.
5. The percussion section always shows up late to rehearsal.
6. Tiffany Chung keeps challenging me every week, thus wasting valuable rehearsal time.
7. Samuel Kwon is always arguing with our

conductor about the bowings for the cello section.

8. Gossip Central (aka The Back of the Second Violin Section) can't concentrate during rehearsal because our second trombonist was caught cheating on his violist girlfriend during break with the first clarinetist.

9. For some reason, we are missing a flute player.

10. Everyone has given up hope that I will be able to play the entire cadenza from memory without making a mistake.

A Typical Thanksgiving Dinner in My House

ME: Please pass the mashed potatoes.

MOM: I know you've been busy with your SAT practice tests, but what about your practice AP tests in English, calculus, economics, Latin?

ME: Can I have more gravy, please?

DAD: What happened in your math class? How could you get a B plus on that test?

ME: Mom, why do you always serve turkey with kimchi?

DAD: I don't understand. We spent four hours on transcendental functions that night.

MOM: You never talk about AP economics. You still have an A in it, right?

ME: I mean, I like kimchi, but I like it with rice and *mandoo* and *bulgogi*. Not with mashed potatoes and roast turkey.

DAD: We should review your calculus test. Let me see what you did wrong.

ME: Oh my God. Is this turkey stuffing made
    with Spam?

MOM: Have you finished your college application
    essays yet?

ME: And why do you always serve these tiny
    dried-up Korean fish sardine things? They're
    super salty. Why can't we have candied yams
    or cranberry sauce?

MOM: I saw a new SAT prep book at the store.
    Do you want me to buy it for you?

ME: No offense, but the kimchi smells. Can I
    move it to the other end of the table?

DAD: Maybe you can ask your teacher if you can
    take a makeup calculus test. A B plus!
    Everyone was talking about it in church! You
    can't afford to slip like this.

MOM: Don't forget to practice the Mendelssohn
    after dinner.

DAD: That's right, the concert is next week.

ME: I'm feeling tired. Can I please be excused?

MOM: Finish your kimchi first.

"No Peace"

My bow seems to melt in my right hand, becoming an extension of my arm as I begin the first twenty-four measures of the Mendelssohn Violin Concerto in E Minor. The opening melody is played entirely on the E string and is really challenging to play in tune. One tiny slip and the music falls apart. It's like walking on a tightrope with no safety net.

I get into the zone immediately. I'm focused, and each note is perfect. As I play, I remember how Mendelssohn was only nine years old when he decided he wanted to write a violin concerto. (Yes, another child prodigy.) It took him seven years before he finally finished it. In fact, he was so frustrated with it that he almost quit. He had written to a friend that the melody gave him "no peace." He even felt embarrassed for taking so long to write it. During my last lesson before tonight's concert, Mr. Mishkind told me that a discouraged Mendelssohn had admitted to his friends, "I feel ashamed . . . but I cannot help it."

Remembering all this helps me feel the true emotion behind the music. Of course the opening melody gave Mendelssohn no peace—it's haunting and poignant. The entire concerto is filled with tension, with its sweeping lines and complex rhythms. And knowing that this composer felt just as frustrated as I do makes me feel better too.

As I near the cadenza, my throat closes. I have had so much trouble memorizing this part of the concerto. I glance into the audience and spot Ben in the front row. I remember how Ben said he didn't care if I played any wrong notes during our jam sessions. I think about how much I've improved in improvising melodies and harmonies on the spot just by listening and thinking on my feet.

I realize—if I make a mistake right now, it won't

matter. I can simply improvise or harmonize until I get to the next measure. I have never felt so calm while playing the cadenza.

I finish the cadenza. No mistakes! No memory slips! I take a deep breath. I look out at my parents sitting in the front row. They're not smiling, but that's not because they disapprove of my performance. My mom and dad never smile during my performances, because they're always terrified I might make a mistake. Sometimes I think they're the ones with stage fright, not me.

Seeing them reminds me of the future. An overwhelming wave of sadness sweeps through my body as it finally sinks in that this is my final solo violin performance of my high-school life. Will there be more concerts after graduation, or is this it? Imagining a future without music feels and looks empty and dark. Now I finally understand what Mendelssohn meant by "no peace."

I focus back on Ben. He's smiling. The red light blinks from the digital recorder in his hands. I'm so grateful he insisted on recording this concert. He's right—I should apply to Juilliard. I'll ask Ben after the concert if I can record the other pieces required for my audition CD at his house during our next rehearsal. I won't tell my parents. I'll take that chance. Besides, Ben said if I get accepted, my parents will be happy and won't care that I lied to them this whole time. I continue to play the Mendelssohn, my violin light in my hands, the stage spotlight gleaming against its beautiful varnished surface, blinding me momentarily.

Top Ten Things I Did Over My Christmas Break

1. Filled out my HarvardYalePrincetonBrown-
   ColumbiaCornellDartmouthPenn college
   applications.
2. Wrote my HarvardYalePrincetonBrown-
   ColumbiaCornellDartmouthPenn college essays.
3. Took an SAT practice test every day and scored
   between a 2200 and 2350 every time.
4. Called Susan every night to talk about how cute
   Ben is.
5. Ate a lot of Spam and kimchi.
6. Practiced the Bach E Major Partita and Paganini
   Caprice for two hours every day.
7. Bought the latest *TEEN POP!* special Christmas
   issue featuring Jet Pack on the cover.
8. Secretly recorded the Bach and Paganini at Ben's
   house using his cool computer program. We
   listened to the recording afterward. Wow! It
   does sound like I'm in a concert hall!
9. Convinced Samuel Kwon to drive me to the

post office so I could secretly mail out my
Juilliard application and audition CD along
with my HarvardYalePrincetonBrownColumbia-
CornellDartmouthPenn applications.

10. Oh yeah . . . Christmas. Kyung Hee's gifts to
our church youth group? Yale sweatshirts. My
parents are thrilled—the Yale sweatshirt matches
their gifts for me: Harvard pajamas and a
Princeton blanket. Bah, humbug!

Amazing

It's 10:30 A.M. on a Saturday. Samuel sits in the car, waiting for me outside the post office. I shift my weight from one foot to the other, waiting my turn in line, clutching nine college application packages. My fingers trace the outline of the CD case packed inside the Juilliard envelope.

Finally it's my turn. I slide the envelopes through the window opening to the postal clerk. As she weighs everything for postage, I start to panic. Why am I applying to Juilliard? Maybe I should stick to the plan and give up the violin after graduation. Maybe I should ask for the Juilliard application back. Come to think of it, why am I applying to all these Ivies as well? What if I don't get in? Oh my God, what am I doing? Am I crazy?

"That'll be fifty-five ninety," the postal clerk says, startling me.

It's not too late for me to change my mind. I hesitate.

And then I hear Ben's voice in my head. *"Patti, you're amazing."*

Ben doesn't care what my SAT scores are and he doesn't judge me by my test scores and grades. He thinks I have cute curly hair, he thinks I'm a talented violinist, he thinks I'm so smart that I can write my own ticket, and he laughs at my stupid jokes.

And if Ben can see all that in me, then maybe I shouldn't be second-guessing myself right now. I hand over the money to the postal clerk. She places the applications in a nearby postal bin. Another postal worker wheels everything away, and once again my future is in someone else's hands.

Remember, a positive attitude can increase one's test scores by several points.

30. Her scholarly rigor and capacity for _____ enabled her to undertake research projects that less _____ people would have found too difficult and tedious.

(A) fanaticism . . . earnest
(B) comprehension . . . indolent
(C) avarice . . . generous
(D) negligence . . . dedicated
(E) concentration . . . disciplined

I know. I know. What are the odds that this question from Practice SAT Test #3 I took back at the end of the summer would be the last question on the official SAT?

It's the first Saturday in January and I'm almost done taking the SATs . . . hopefully for the last time. I remember my SAT Tips of the Day, and I don't waste time as I darken the circle next to (E).

I glance at the clock. 12:58 P.M. Two more minutes, and the test proctor will announce, "Pencils down."

Black lead marks cover my fingertips. The earthy scent of pencil eraser dust fills the air. My neck and back are sore from sitting down all morning, hunched over my desk, filling in a thousand little circles next to an endless stream of SAT questions.

"Pencils down." It's one o'clock.

I put my pencil down.

Harvard Alumni Interviewers Are Human Beings, Too! Part 1

"What are your academic strengths and weaknesses?" Samuel asks.

"I'm pretty good at humanities, like AP English," I say. "I guess AP Calc's my hardest subject."

"*No!* You *never* say you're 'pretty good' at anything!"

"And don't forget, never admit you have any weaknesses," Tiffany adds.

"Sorry," I say.

"Let's try this one," Samuel says, sitting down again. "How did you first hear about Harvard?"

"My parents."

"No!" Everyone shouts. It's two o'clock on Sunday, and my church youth group is practicing college alumni interviews.

I'm up first because my Harvard alumni interview is next week. So far I've blown it on every single question:

SAMUEL (pretending to be the Harvard alumni interviewer): What have you read most recently? Did it make an impression on you? The way you think? Your approach to life?

ME: I liked Sartre's *No Exit*. There's this line in the play that reminds me of my high school.

SAMUEL (curious): Really? What line would that be?

ME: "Hell is other people."

SAMUEL: Patti! Come on, be *serious*!

ME: I *am* being serious.

And so on. You get the picture. Finally Samuel can't take it any longer. He opens his backpack and pulls out a book with the title (I'm not kidding) *Only the Best and the Brightest—Achieving Acceptance into the Ivy League*. He opens the book and hands it to me.

"Read page two eleven," he says.

I read out loud: "'Remember, Harvard alumni interviewers are human beings, too! Keep reminding yourself that the interviewer sitting across from you is an ordinary person, since this will help you to relax and view your interviewer in the right context. Think of him or her as a good adult friend or relative.'"

"I don't know about that, Samuel," I say, shutting the book. "I don't have any good adult friends. And thinking of the Harvard alumni interviewer as a relative of mine may not be such a great idea."

Samuel shakes his head. "Patti, trust The Book," he says, his voice hushed and reverent. "Be honest . . ."

". . . but not too honest," Tiffany says.

"Don't forget to speak intelligently," Isaac adds.

"But be coherent," Sally says.

"Think of them as your best friend," Samuel says.

"Are you sure?" I ask.

He smiles. "Of course I'm sure. If it's in The Book, then it's right. You should borrow it." He holds it up.

I hesitate, then decide, why not? It can't hurt.

"Okay," I say, stuffing the book into my backpack. "Harvard alumni interviewers are human, too." I take a deep breath and smile back. After all, how hard can a college alumni interview be?

Harvard Alumni Interviewers Are Human Beings, Too!
Part 2

Harvard alumni interviewers are human beings, too, I keep thinking as Wilton Turchi, Esq., Harvard class of 1974, wipes a speck of dust from his wire-rimmed glasses.

It's Wednesday night around eight o'clock, and we've been talking for about an hour in the living room while my parents hover in the kitchen, pretending not to eavesdrop on our interview.

Anyway, despite what Samuel and his stupid college guidebook say, it's impossible for me to think of Wilton Turchi, Esq., as a "good adult friend" or relative. He went to Harvard as an undergraduate and then went to Harvard again as a law student. He is now a partner in Barnhardt, Maristed, Silber & Edwards, a law firm in Hartford.

During my interview, Mr. Turchi asks all the questions that Samuel's college guidebook said college interviewers would ask: *Why do you want to attend Harvard? What is your strongest/weakest point? Tell me about your interests. What has been your greatest experience in high school? Who is your favorite author, and why?*

The night before my interview, I went ahead and prepared my answers. But as I answer each one of Mr. Turchi's queries, I make sure to sound as unrehearsed as possible so I can thus "engage the college interviewer in a two-way dynamic dialogue." (That's what The Book says.) I do my best to make our dialogue as dynamic as possible. *I like Harvard's rigorous and challenging academic program, especially its English department. My strongest point is that I work very hard. My weakest point is that I'm very ambitious and sometimes I take on too many projects, but because I work hard, I always manage to finish these projects. My favorite author is Jane Austen because of her sharp and witty observations of society's pressure on young women to do as they're told and not to rock the boat.*

But so far Mr. Turchi looks really bored. I start to panic.

And then Mr. Turchi throws me a curveball. "Tell me about your family."

I'm completely speechless.

He tries again. "Your parents are from Korea. Why did they move here? What have you learned from them?"

I did not prepare an answer for this question. Nowhere in The Book did it say that Harvard alumni interviewers would ask applicants about their family. What does my family have to do with getting into Harvard?

"My dad is . . . he works . . . he makes software for banks and . . . stuff." Stuff? Come on, Patti. Focus! "My mom . . . she, well . . . she's a pharmacist and . . ." I just stop talking. I figure less is more.

"Interesting," Mr. Turchi says, but he doesn't look interested. "What are they like? Would you say you act more like your mother or father? Or both?"

What are they like? As in their personalities? "They are a hard-working people," I say, suddenly sounding like a pompous narrator for those *National Geographic* TV documentary specials, on, say, the herding habits of gazelles. "They want the best for me. They have inspired me to work hard and be the best at everything I do. . . ."

"I think all parents want the best for their children, don't you agree?" Mr. Turchi says, not buying my fake monologue.

"They put a lot of pressure on me." Oh my God. Where did that come from? I shut my mouth.

But Mr. Turchi finally looks interested. "Really?" He laughs. "I know what that's like."

"Tell me about it," I blurt out loud. To my relief, Mr. Turchi is still smiling.

"My parents would get upset about any grade I brought home that was below an A minus," he says, his tone casual, as if we were just friends.

"A minus?" I blurt out. "You were lucky. Me, I can't get anything below an A or I bring shame not only to my family but to my entire Korean church."

Mr. Turchi chuckles. "Now that's a burden to carry."

"I know!" All of sudden, the words pour out of me and I can't stop myself. I tell Mr. Turchi about my dad studying fourteen hours a day in his *hagwon* to pass the college entrance exams, how he brought shame on his family for failing, about how competitive everyone is in my Korean church youth group and how Samuel is going to SAT boot camp *twice* and how my mom thinks being smart is much more valuable than being beautiful but that's easy for her to say because she *is* both smart and beautiful.

When I finish, Mr. Turchi smiles. "Thank you for being so honest and candid, Patti," he says. "Your cultural viewpoint is very illuminating." He jots down a few notes on a small pad of paper.

I relax. Yes! I saved my alumni interview from becoming a disaster.

Unfortunately Mr. Turchi isn't done with my interview. "I have one last question," he says. "What do you want to do for the future?"

What do I want to do for the future? How could I have not anticipated this question? It's so obvious—I can't believe I forgot to prepare an answer for this one. But I'm sure I can improvise something clever on the spot.

Instead I open my mouth but no words come out. What's wrong with me? *Say something.*

Mr. Turchi's smile fades. "Patti?" He asks. "What's your answer?"

I must say something, anything at this point, or my Harvard alumni interview will go up in flames. "Isn't that why I'm applying to Harvard?" I say in desperation. "To find out what I want to do for the future."

Judging from the disappointed look on Mr. Turchi's face, I had better do really well on the SATs if I want to get into Harvard. Obviously Samuel's college guidebook was wrong—Harvard alumni interviewers are *not* human, because otherwise they would make mistakes just like the rest of us.

Jet Pack U.S. Tour Dates—East Coast

From the Jet Pack official website:

JET PACK NATIONAL TOUR DATES:
Feb. 11—Warner Theatre, Washington, DC
Feb. 12—Sovereign Performing Arts Center,
       Reading, PA
Feb. 15—Borgata Hotel Casino & Spa,
       Atlantic City, NJ
Feb. 19—Madison Square Garden,
       New York, NY
Feb. 21—Fox Theatre, Mashantucket, CT

Tickets for Jet Pack are on sale right now. I sit at my computer, frantically hitting the return key on the ticket website. But every time I hit return, the words *server is busy* appear onscreen. I also keep dialing the 1-800 ticket line, but the phone line is busy, too. *Why can't I get through?!* As if I don't have enough to stress about with my upcoming Princeton and Yale alumni interviews, spring semester classes, Lock-In in February, Juilliard, All-State in April, AP exams in May, and holding on to my valedictorian status for graduation!

Why am I even bothering to buy Jet Pack tickets? As if my parents would let me drive all the way out to Mashantucket to see a rock band by myself. I should be studying, but frankly, this is much more important. I'm going to be valedictorian—surely I can figure out a smart strategy for convincing my parents to let me see Jet Pack in concert.

My computer beeps. Finally! I got through!

Oh no. "Sold out."

What? Tickets have only been on sale for *five minutes*. It's not fair! I do nothing but study all the time! I get straight As! I practice my violin three hours every day! I go to church every Sunday and don't complain! And do I get any reward for all my hard work? Like one measly little ticket to see Jet Pack in concert? Nope! Nothing! Why do I even bother?

I slump back in my chair. Who cares if I get into *HARVARDYALEPRINCETON* or Juilliard? Jet Pack has sold out. My life has no meaning anymore.

Fun

"So what do you like to do for fun?"

What? Fun? I'm being interviewed by Sandy
Yardumian, Princeton class of 1987, for my Princeton
alumni college interview. She majored in economics
and works as a financial consultant in Hartford.

I'm a little stumped by her question. Is it a trick
question? If I tell her I don't have time for fun because
I'm too busy studying, she might think I'm too one-
dimensional and not a diverse enough candidate for
Princeton. But if I tell her about what I like to do for
fun (and I'm not even sure what that is), then she might

think I'm not serious enough about college.

"What about music?" she asks after a few moments of silence. "You have an impressive musical background. What musicians do you like?"

"Mendelssohn," I say. "And Brahms, Mozart, Bach . . ."

She smiles. "Of course you like classical music. What about other types of music? Are there any bands you like?"

I hesitate. What kind of question is this? "Jet Pack's my favorite band," I finally say.

Ms. Yardumian laughs. "I like Jet Pack, too! My oldest daughter is thirteen. She has all their albums."

"So do I," I say. It feels awkward, talking about Jet Pack with my Princeton alumni interviewer, but I'm kind of relieved not to be answering questions about my favorite author and where I see myself ten years from now.

"Who's your favorite?" she asks. Her eyes gleam, and she leans forward eagerly. Even though she's much older than me, her voice takes on this really youthful vibe.

"I like . . ."

"Oh! Let me guess. Simon?"

I smile. "You like him, too?"

"He reminds me of John Taylor."

"Who's John Taylor?" I ask. "Is he Simon's brother?"

"No. It's a coincidence that they have the same last name. There was this band called Duran Duran that I worshipped when I was in high school. John Taylor was their bassist."

I quickly calculate how long ago this was—Ms. Yardumian graduated in 1987, which means she was my age in 1983. My mix CD from Ben is filled with what he called "old school" bands from the late seventies and early eighties. "So Duran Duran is really old school," I say.

She laughs. "That's so funny, Patti. Exactly! Old school. You should check out their CDs. If you like Jet Pack, then you'll *love* Duran Duran."

Note to self: Go online and research Duran Duran instead of doing your AP calc homework. Find out if John Taylor is as cute as Simon Taylor. I grin, happy that this college alumni interview is going well. And then . . .

"So what do you want to do in the future?"

I'm better prepared this time to answer. I spent all

last night preparing the perfect response. I even wrote it down and memorized it, just in case: *"I want to be a lawyer, because there is so much injustice in this world, and I want to help others. I believe my assertive behavior coupled with my compassionate nature and keen, intelligent mind make me the perfect candidate to major in prelaw at Princeton."* Okay, I admit, I don't really want to be a lawyer. But Kyung Hee's a lawyer. In fact, practically all the older kids who graduated from our Korean church youth group have become either lawyers or doctors, so I figured it would be a safe answer.

"I want to be a lawyer," I say.

"Why?" she asks.

"Because there's so much injustice in this world, and I want to help others." So far so good. I'm speaking in a natural, conversational tone, and she's asking me specific questions. We are definitely engaged in a dynamic conversation, which is a good thing according to Samuel's stupid *Only the Best and the Brightest— Achieving Acceptance into the Ivy League. (Going in too stiff and intent only on reciting your accomplishments and your memorized list of the benefits of going to college is a sure recipe for disaster. Try to engage in DYNAMIC CONVERSATION rather than stiff Q&A.)*

"So you're interested in litigation."

Oh no. I didn't say what type of law I wanted to specialize in—courtroom trials, tort law, contracts. Do I want to be a defense lawyer or a prosecutor? I recite my paragraph, putting a halt to our dynamic conversation: "I want to help others. I believe my assertive behavior coupled with my compassionate nature and keen, intelligent mind make me the perfect candidate to major in prelaw at Princeton."

Ms. Yardumian jots something down in her small spiral notebook. "Interesting," she says, her voice flat. "Unfortunately Princeton doesn't have a prelaw degree."

No! First Harvard, now Princeton. Why is everyone so concerned about my future? Why am I having so much trouble answering such a simple question?

Prove My Love, Part I

"I got them!" Stephanie rushes into homeroom, waving a piece of a paper in the air. Ben and I stop talking for a moment and watch as Stephanie reaches her desk. She shoves the paper in front of Maura and Erin. There's a moment of silence, and then all three of them squeal.

"Oh my God, you got front-row tickets to Jet Pack!" Erin shouts.

AUUUUUGGGGGGGHHHHHH!!!!!! Jet Pack? Stephanie got tickets to Jet Pack? How? They sold out in less than five minutes! I didn't even know she liked Jet Pack! It's not fair. I bet Stephanie isn't a true fan like me. I bet she doesn't know that Simon Taylor's favorite band growing up was U2 and that he originally studied literature at Cambridge and wanted to be a professor until he started the band. She probably doesn't even know the date of his birthday!

Ben laughs. "Patti, if you could see your expression right now. . . ."

"It's not funny." I pout.

"I'm sorry." Ben tries his best to look sympathetic, but he can't. He grins again. "Come on—I'm disappointed in you. After all those CDs I made for you, and you still prefer this teenybopper bubblegum trendy flash-in-the-pan fake band instead of The Clash?"

"I like The Clash," I say. (It's true. I really do. Ben's CDs have had a profound impact on my musical tastes.) "But Jet Pack . . . see, the reason I . . ."

"I know, you think the lead singer is cute." Ben smiles.

Even though it's really sweet of Ben to comfort me, I'm still in a foul mood now, because Stephanie gets to see Jet Pack and *I don't!*

"Here." Ben leans forward. "I have something that will make you feel better." He slides over a piece of paper.

I pick it up. It's a ticket. "Blister," I read out loud. "Who's that?"

"New British band," Ben explains. "They're really cool. They're doing a show at Toad's Place in New Haven. They're like the Sex Pistols meet the Strokes meet the . . ." He laughs. "You'd like them. Stephanie's not into this type of music, so I thought maybe you'd want to go instead."

I'm simultaneously ecstatic that Ben is asking me to see this band with him and shattered that he thought of Stephanie first, which means that I'm in second place. And you know how we feel about second place in my family.

But when I look into Ben's green eyes, partially hidden by his long bangs that desperately need another trim, my heart skips and goose bumps prickle my arms. Oh, who cares about Stephanie? If I say yes, this means that Ben and I will be going to a concert *by ourselves*. My parents? I'm sure I'll figure out something. I'm not going to ruin this moment by saying no.

"Yes," I say.

"Great! I can drive us down to New Haven."

"Okay." I grab the edge of my desk, because if I

don't, I will float up to the ceiling. I stare at the ticket lying on my desk. I can't believe Ben just asked me out. I'm so happy, I don't care about Jet Pack right now and . . .

Oh no!

I'm looking at the date printed at the top of the ticket. BLISTER—ALL AGES SHOW—TOAD'S PLACE—SATURDAY FEBRUARY 14.

Saturday February 14?

That's the same date as our church youth group Lock-In.

All The Time in the World

This time, Jane Bright, Yale class of 1991, visits our house.

When I heard about her background, I wanted to bang my head against the wall—high school class valedictorian, perfect SAT scores, and a summa cum laude double degree in chemistry and physics at Yale.

For the past hour I haven't messed up. She smiles at all my answers about my favorite class (AP English), why I prefer physics to chemistry (I love the poetry behind Newton's Three Laws of Motion), and even laughs when I tell her some funny stories about my church youth group.

We're near the end of the interview when I realize I haven't asked Jane about herself. "So what did you do after graduating from Yale?" I ask, trying to show an interest in her life because The Book says that's what you're supposed to do in a successful college interview.

To my surprise, Jane doesn't say something like "I went to medical school" or "I worked at Dow Chemical as a researcher."

Instead she says, "I became a musician."

What?!

She smiles and points to my neck. "You're a violinist—I can tell by that." She's pointing to a permanent scar on the left side of my neck, my "violin mark," which is the result of years of pressing my violin against my neck. It's like a badge of honor—the more you practice, the more visible your violin mark.

"Do you play violin?" I ask.

"Piano."

"Why didn't you major in music at Yale or go to music school?" I ask.

"My parents were afraid that majoring in music was too uncertain," she says. "They wanted me to have a solid chance at getting a job, so they pushed me toward the sciences. I was planning on med school after graduation, but at the last minute I decided to pursue my master's degree in piano performance at Juilliard instead."

"Oh my God, my parents would *kill* me if I did that," I say before I can stop myself. I gasp and place my hand over my mouth. "Sorry," I mumble.

Ms. Bright smiles. "You're right. My parents were furious. But I had to start living my life for myself. Now I'm a professional freelance musician and I teach private music lessons to children. It's not a lot of money and it's a tough life, but I'm happy. Doesn't music make you happy?"

"This might sound strange," I say slowly, "but I feel safe when I play the violin. Everything disappears, and all that matters is the music. Does that make sense?"

"Perfectly." She jots down something in her notebook and then stands up. "Patti, I think you would make an *excellent* Yale candidate. I'm going to write up a very strong recommendation for you. I also highly recommend that you apply for Yale's special music program for incoming freshmen. That way you can still study music no matter what you decide to major in."

I walk Ms. Bright to the front door. Before she leaves, I say. "Excuse me. Can I ask you one more question?"

"Of course."

I glance around to make sure my parents haven't snuck up behind us to eavesdrop. I lower my voice. "What was Juilliard like?"

"Did you apply there too?"

"Yes."

"I loved Juilliard," she says. "But I'm glad I went there for graduate school instead. I needed four years of college to figure out what I really wanted to do." She laughs. "Want to hear something weird? There's now a part of me that is thinking about going to medical school in a few years."

"For your parents?" I ask.

"No," she says. "For myself. I've been researching music therapy and medicine, and I think there's a way to combine my love for music with my science background." She shrugs. "I'm in no hurry, though. I've got all the time in the world." She looks me in the eye.

"You know that, right? You've got all the time in the world, Patti."

Even though this is the first and only time I've met Ms. Bright, there's something in her voice that makes me want desperately to believe her with all my heart.

The Sixth Commandment

"You lied *twice*?" Samuel's eyes widen. "You broke the sixth commandment."

"I didn't kill anyone," I snap. "Bearing false witness is the *ninth* commandment."

"So you still broke one. Actually, you broke two. You're supposed to honor your mother and father."

"As far as I'm concerned, the fifth commandment doesn't count because they don't honor me." I now regret confiding in Samuel Kwon.

We are tacking up red streamers across the church rec room for Valentine's Day.

Everyone's pretty stressed, and tempers are flaring

over the stupidest mistakes. (Isaac dropped a bottle of glitter all over the carpet and Tiffany yelled at him, saying he was so stupid that it was no wonder he was going to graduate without having taken any math class past trigonometry. "What kind of honors student graduates with only *three* years of math?" she asked. We were all horrified by the depth of her insult, but at the same time we were also horrified that Isaac had taken only three, and not four, years of math.)

Anyway, Samuel seemed a little preoccupied because he kept dropping the tacks. I asked him what was wrong, and he suddenly started confessing his whole life to me, about how he's sick of his parents bothering him about college and how he just found out that he is *not* valedictorian but salutatorian of his class. Of course I gave him a moment of respectful silence. Then he asked me if I wanted to carpool with him to the Lock-In and I said no, and before I could stop myself, I blurted out, "Ben and I are seeing Blister that night but my parents don't know about it." And Samuel snapped. "What's wrong with you, Patti? You've changed so much. You never used to cause trouble. And what kind of name is Blister, anyway?"

I hand Samuel another tack.

"It's getting out of hand," he continues. "You're lying to your parents all the time now."

"Patti lied to her parents?" Sally looks up from the other side of the room, where she's been fiddling with the TV to get better reception. "About what?"

Before I can stop him, Samuel blurts out, "Patti applied to Juilliard without telling her parents."

Tiffany accidentally cuts a pink construction paper heart in half and frowns. "Patti, if they find out, you are so totally in trouble."

"I think it's kind of cool," Isaac says. I almost fall off the stepladder. Isaac *never* talks, much less expresses an opinion.

"I think Patti should do what she wants," Isaac continues. "She's the best violinist in the whole state."

"And what about you?" Tiffany asks, her voice sharp. I think she must still be mad at Isaac for spilling the glitter. "Are you doing what you want?"

Isaac shrugs. "Of course not. Are you?"

"Of course I am," Tiffany says, her voice faltering.

"Right," Isaac says. "See, none of us are doing what we *really* want. But Patti has a gift. She's got a chance that we don't. So if she wants to apply to Juilliard without her parents' permission, well, I say, go for it."

I stare at Isaac with his choppy short hair, thick eyeglasses, and too-short pants revealing mismatched socks. Of course he's the guy who gets stuffed into the lockers at his school. Of course he's a grade-A nerd who has to cover his test with his entire arm so no one can copy his answers. But right now, as he stands in the middle of our rec room clutching a bottle of Elmer's glue, Isaac has never looked so strong and self-assured.

"I agree," Sally pipes up. "Patti, you have to tell us what happens next." There's this light in her eyes and an eagerness in her voice that I've never heard before.

"I don't know," Tiffany says, her voice doubtful. "If Harvard accepts you, you don't turn them down."

"Patti's also going to see a rock band in New Haven," Samuel says. "Her parents don't know about that, either."

I seriously consider alternatives to the sixth commandment ("Thou shalt not commit murder") because *I am going to kill Samuel Kwon.*

"Technically speaking, I haven't lied," I explain. "I just haven't said anything to them."

"How are you getting to this concert?" Tiffany asks.

"Ben's picking me up," I say.

"Ben?" Lisa asks. "Who's Ben?"

Suddenly everyone all speaks at once. "What does he look like?" "Are you guys going out?" "When's the concert?"

"He looks like Simon Taylor from Jet Pack. No, we're not dating. The band plays this Saturday in New Haven."

"You can't go," Samuel says. "That's when we have our Lock-In."

"I know," I say, staring him down.

There's a moment of silence as the collective brainpower in the room (three class valedictorians, one salutatorian, and a Siemens Competition winner) whirs and clicks until it dawns on everyone that *I don't plan to be at this year's Lock-In!*

Sally gasps. "But you're in charge of the scavenger hunt!"

"Oh please," I say. "Come on, does anyone here really want to run around the church looking for stupid things on a list?"

After a painfully long moment of silence, Isaac

raises his hand. "So how are you going to pull this off?"

"I don't know," I say. "But you guys are going to help me."

The atmosphere in the room has changed. There's electricity in the air as everyone surrounds me. I have the sneaking suspicion they rather like my secret rebellion.

"Tell us everything," Tiffany says. "Don't skimp on the details."

I start from the beginning. As we finish decorating the church rec room with red-and-white crepe paper streamers and lopsided construction-paper hearts, my entire church youth group now knows the whole story—how I met Ben at the All-State auditions and how he and I secretly wrote songs together and traded CDs, and how he asked me out but he also asked Stephanie out and I have no idea if they are officially a couple or not.

"She sounds like an airhead," Tiffany says after I describe Stephanie to them. "You say she's had only two years of math? What a ditz."

"You have to play us that CD Ben made for you," Sally says.

Even Samuel stops lecturing me. "I'm not happy with your deception," he says, "but I think you should do it. The odds are in your favor of convincing this guy to go for you and not Stephanie because you clearly share more mutual interests."

As I continue to answer everyone's questions about Ben and Juilliard, I notice that they're hanging on to my every word. They're going through the same kind of agony and pressure that I'm going through. I think about Tiffany and her love for dance, but how her parents want her to study economics at Smith. Samuel may be a math genius, but I know he'd rather go to California instead of MIT and work for a movie special-effects company in Hollywood. I've become their champion, the one who gets to go out on a date. Even though it's not really a date and even though I'm not Ben's girlfriend, if it's good enough for my Korean church youth group, then it's certainly good enough for me.

Good Eyes

"Close your eyes. Good. Now, open them."

There's a moment of silence as Tiffany, Sally, and Lisa examine me. Susan, whom I invited to Lock-In as my guest, stands by the door, on guard duty for Kyung Hee.

Tiffany, Sally, and Lisa exchange glances.

"Yeah," Tiffany says, sighing. "She doesn't have them."

"Have what?" I peer into the mirror. I am blind as a bat without my eyeglasses, so I have to lean about an inch from the mirror to see my face clearly. From what I can tell, it looks like my eyelids are slathered in a deep cerulean shade of blue. It's like someone took a bright-blue Magic Marker and smeared it across my eyelids.

It's Saturday night and we're huddled in the church bathroom. Our parents dropped us all off at noon at the church, where Kyung Hee was waiting. We spent the afternoon in Bible Study, capped off with a rousing game of Bible Pictionary (which I won again, thank you very much). Then we took over the church kitchen and had a pizza party.

It's now a few minutes before eight o'clock, and we're supposed to be in the rec room doing the ice cream sundae bar before settling down to watch a couple movie rentals. I have to admit, this year's Lock-In has been more fun than I had anticipated.

Samuel surprised me by coming up with the main plan of how to sneak me out of the church. He convinced Kyung Hee that the infamous scavenger hunt should take place after we watch the movie rentals, not before. During the ice cream sundae bar activity, I would sneak outside and wait for Ben to pick up me at eight o'clock as planned. Samuel figured the ice cream sundae bar was going to be a messy affair, and that Kyung Hee would be so distracted, she wouldn't notice my absence.

He also planned to turn the lights off during the movie rental activity so Kyung Hee would not see I was missing. He instructed Susan to keep Kyung Hee preoccupied with questions about Jesus so I could sneak back into the church without her noticing. And voilà! I'd return just in time for all of us to go online and check our January SAT scores (they were being released at midnight on the SAT website). And then I'd lead everyone in the scavenger hunt.

I was pretty impressed. But Samuel just shrugged. "I play Star Wars Galaxies online every night with thousands of other gamers," he explained. "I'm third in command on my Imperial Starship. I'm all about the strategy."

But as I was sneaking down the hallway with Susan as my wingman, Tiffany, Lisa, and Sally appeared out of nowhere. Tiffany grabbed my arm. "You can't go out like that," she hissed, dragging us to the bathroom, insisting it would take only a few minutes to make me look more presentable.

Yeah. Presentable all right. Only if I were going to a Halloween Masquerade Ball. I raise my hand to my eyes.

"Don't rub it off," Sally says, grabbing my hand before I can swipe away at this horrible makeup.

230

"What did you do to me?" I wail. "I look awful."

"Your eyelid's supposed to fold up," Tiffany says. "Like this, see?" She closes her eyes so I can see her blue eye-shadowed eyelids. When she opens them, the skin folds over so the blue is a tasteful rim above her eye.

"I don't have good eyes," I say. "You should know that. My eyelids don't fold like that. They just sit there."

"How do you put on eye makeup?" Lisa asks.

"I don't wear makeup."

There's a collective gasp of horror.

"Are you going to have the operation?" Tiffany asks. "I got mine done last year."

"No way!" I snap.

"What are you guys talking about?" Susan asks, glancing every now and then down the hallway, keeping guard. "What operation?"

"It's called blepharoplasty," I explain. "Basically they cut into your eyelid to create a fold."

Susan makes a face. "That's disgusting. Why would anyone do that?"

I shrug. "Pressure from society?"

"Patti, your eyes are fine," Susan says. "There's nothing wrong with them."

"Here." Tiffany pulls out her tube of bright-red lipstick. "This'll take away the attention from your eyes."

Sally puts my glasses back on. "That's better, too. Your frames hide a lot of the blue."

"You need more styling gel," Lisa suggests, dipping her fingers into a glass jar of hair gel. She slicks my hair back on the sides. This stuff dries so quickly that when I press the sides of my head, I can hear my hair crunch. At least it's been a few months since the Body Wave Perm Incident, and most of the curls have straightened out.

"I know!" Sally squeals. "With her Harry Potter glasses, we should put her hair in pigtails!" Sally and Tiffany attack my hair, and in less than five minutes I have two long braided pigtails spilling past my shoulders.

"And now for your outfit," Tiffany says, reaching under a sink for a plastic shopping bag. She pulls out several items, the tags still on. She holds up a pair of faded blue jeans and shakes her head. Then she finds a cute red-plaid schoolgirl skirt and claps her hands.

"You are so going to be punk rock schoolgirl," she says, throwing the skirt at me. "You've already got the schoolgirl top," she adds, nodding at the white button-down blouse I'm wearing. "Who dresses you, your mom?"

"Of course," I say, puzzled, taking off my jeans and putting on the skirt.

"Wait." And then Tiffany does the unthinkable. She's wearing this really cute black top, a shimmery slip of a tank top with spaghetti straps and black lace along the neckline. She simply takes it off, and stands there in nothing but her jeans and strapless bra.

I look away, embarrassed. "Tiffany, what are you doing?" I say.

"We don't have time. Put this on."

"But my bra will show through," I say.

Tiffany smiles. "You're not wearing a bra."

She tosses the top at me. I turn around and take off my blouse and bra and slip the top over me. It feels light and smooth and silky against my skin and fits snugly against my chest.

"I don't know why you dress like such a dork," Tiffany says, taking my blouse and throwing it into a nearby wastebasket.

"Tiffany! That's not very nice," Lisa says.

"Patti knows what I mean." Tiffany sighs. "I meant it in a good way. Look at how tiny her waist is."

They all look at me. I cross my arms, embarrassed. "You guys . . ." I begin.

Tiffany snaps her fingers at Sally. "Boots."

"But these are my favorite . . ."

"Boots. Now. You're both a size five."

Sally sighs and takes off her black leather knee-high boots. I kick off my shoes and put on her boots. Tiffany swings me toward the full-length mirror against the back wall. "See?" She smiles proudly. "Less is more. All you need are the right accessories."

Susan gasps and rushes toward me, the bathroom door closing behind her. "Patti, you look so cute!" she says.

You know, I have to admit Susan's right. I do look pretty good. I didn't realize my waist was so tiny either. I guess it's because I'm always obsessed with my chunky thighs. But this top and my new school-girl skirt create the illusion that I've actually got a nice figure. With my pigtails and bright-red lipstick, I look sort of, well . . . *sexy*. For some reason my face doesn't look as fat, and my nose isn't so flat. In fact, my face looks kind of cute and heart shaped. I smile at my reflection.

"Total rocker chick!" Sally says, giggling. "Patti, we have to go shopping next weekend and get you a whole new wardrobe."

"You are so *Kill Bill*, but in a good way," Tiffany says. "Now, if only we had some—"

The door swings open. It's Kyung Hee.

Tiffany gasps. Sally makes a little "Oh!" squeal. Lisa drops the jar of hair gel, the glass shattering on impact.

"I was wondering where you girls were . . ." Kyung Hee slowly takes in the scene before her—Tiffany's makeup kit in the sink, the hair gel on the floor, me in my Catholic-schoolgirl-gone-bad getup.

"What the hell is going on?" she snaps.

I don't know what's scarier—us getting in trouble or Kyung Hee swearing.

"We were just fooling around," Tiffany says.

"We lost track of time," Sally offers.

"We were just—" Lisa begins.

"Is it time for the ice cream sundae bar?" Susan asks.

"Stop." Kyung Hee raises her hands. "I'm not stupid."

I look down at the floor.

"How could you do this?" Kyung Hee says to me. "We worked so hard to make this Lock-In a success."

In my mind, I see Ben driving up to the front of the church, wondering why I'm not outside like I said. I can see Ben waiting another minute before giving up and leaving, and me running out the front door, too late as the car peels out of the driveway.

No. I have not suffered this much to let Kyung Hee prevent me from spending what will probably be the best night of my life. I shake my head.

"No," I say. "I'm not staying. Ben is picking me up. We're seeing Blister tonight."

"Ben?" Kyung Hee's eyes narrow. "Who's Ben?"

"He's her boyfriend," Lisa says.

"Well, not really her boyfriend, like boyfriend *boyfriend*," Sally says.

"He has no idea she likes him," Tiffany says.

"And he might be dating Stephanie." Susan makes a face.

Kyung Hee raises her hands again. "Stop. I can't hear anything when you all talk at once." The corners of her mouth twitch, as if she's struggling to keep from smiling. "If you think high school is all about the drama, just wait until you're my age. Instead of hearing about SATs and *HARVARDYALEPRINCETON*, they'll be pressuring you to get married, and preferably to a nice Korean doctor."

She tugs one of my pigtails. "The girls did a good job on you. All you need is this final touch."

And then Kyung Hee grabs a can of hairspray sitting in the sink and smoothes away my flyaways. "Just be back before dawn," she says softly.

Prove My Love, Part 2

The temperature has dropped. I shiver as I stand outside the church, waiting for Ben. I tug at the hem of my skirt, not used to wearing something so short. I find a loose thread and yank it. It unravels even more. I bend over to grab it with both hands.

I'm still bent over, trying to snap the thread in half, when Ben pulls up the driveway. I let go of the thread and stand up. He leans over and opens the passenger door. "Hey, Patti, you ready?"

I enter the car and shut the door. "Yeah, I can't wait."

Ben turns on the car stereo, loud crunchy rock

music blaring from the speakers. "This is Blister!" he shouts.

It's a pretty cool song, just a simple verse-chorus-verse setup with a lot of feedback and distortion. Suddenly I hear a high-pitched squeal. "Is that a violin?" I ask.

He smiles. "That's why I thought you'd like this band." We peel out of the driveway.

By the time we reach New Haven, we've listened to the CD twice. The gothic spires and towers of Yale University loom over us as we exit off I-91 and head down York Street toward Toad's Place. I had no idea this club would be right in the heart of the Yale campus.

"Thanks for the surprise college tour," I say.

Ben laughs as he parks the car. The marquee for Toad's Place blinks just a block away. I shiver again. Ben takes off his jacket. "Here," he says, wrapping his jacket over my shoulders. I feel so warm. There are butterflies in my stomach. I look into his beautiful green eyes. "Thanks," I say.

We enter the club. It reeks of cigarette smoke, stale beer, and sweat. But when Ben grabs my hand to guide me through the crowd, this club becomes the most romantic place in the world.

We squeeze past everyone until we find a spot in the middle of the floor. It's a small club, so we stand shoulder to shoulder with everyone. I crane my neck back, trying to get a view of the stage. If the two guys in front of me don't move, I have a tiny view of the middle microphone onstage.

A song blares from the speakers as we wait for the band. I recognize it. "It's The Clash," I shout over the din. Ben smiles at me.

The lights dim. The crowd cheers. The roar is deafening. A spotlight shines on Blister as they walk onstage. It's just three guys—a stocky, barrel-chested guitarist sporting a bowling shirt and long sideburns, along with a tall, gangly, long-haired guy holding a bass and a bald, intense-looking guy sitting behind the drums.

They launch into their first song. All I hear is the pulsing bass and the pounding of the drums. The singer's surly voice pierces the air.

Everyone surges forward. Bodies slam against each other as people dance and throw themselves against each other.

Ben stomps his feet in perfect rhythm to the music,

like a human metronome. He grins at me. The music is infectious, and I find myself bobbing along to the heavy backbeat of the drums. By the third song, I'm hooked.

Then the band plays a slower song. The lead singer picks up an instrument propped against the drum set. It's the violin! I jump up and down, trying to catch glimpses of him playing the violin. He's not the world's greatest violinist, but it doesn't matter. The simple solo floats above the edgy bass line. Ben was right. Less is more in rock. I can't wait for our next rehearsal.

Something tickles against my right thigh. I reach down and find the loose thread from the hem of my skirt. It's almost a foot long. I had better rip this thread off before my whole skirt unravels. I grip the thread with both hands and am about to snap it in half when the band starts a new song. It sounds so familiar.

To my surprise, I recognize the lyrics. It's not an original song—it's a cover version of the Violent Femmes' "Prove My Love," one of the songs Ben burned onto my compilation CD.

Suddenly people push each other in a mad rush to the stage. I lose sight of Ben. I jump up and down, trying to see the band and trying to find Ben.

Someone shoves me. I smack into the guy in front of me. My glasses slip off my left ear, dangling against my face.

"What do I have to do to prove my love to you?" the lead singer shouts.

"Patti!" I turn toward the sound of Ben's voice.

Bam! The guy's elbow smashes my face. My glasses go flying. I slip and fall backward. No one notices I'm lying on the floor. I can't stand up because everyone is rushing the stage and no one sees me. Feet trample all over me. I've never been so terrified in my life.

Ben appears out of nowhere. He pushes the guy in front of me away. "Hey, watch it!" the guy shouts. But Ben doesn't care. He grabs my arm and yanks me back to my feet. "Are you okay?" he shouts, concerned.

"I lost my glasses," I say, and suddenly I burst into tears. I could die right here and now from the humiliation. My skirt's ripped, my pigtails have come undone, and lipstick is smeared across my cheeks—and the lead singer is wailing on about how he would swim the ocean and climb a mountain to prove his love.

"Don't move," Ben says. He turns around and dives into the crowd, disappearing into a sea of limbs. After a few seconds he returns, holding a pair of twisted black frames. "I found them," he shouts.

I grab my glasses. Everything looks blurry because I'm really nearsighted. I hold the glasses right up to my face. They come into focus. I gasp. *No!* The left lens is missing, and the frames are twisted beyond repair.

"Can you see without them?" Ben asks.

I shake my head. I start crying again. It no longer matters if I get accepted into college or not because *my parents are going to kill me.*

Ben uses the sleeve of his jacket to dry my tears. "It's okay," he yells. "At least that jerk didn't break your teeth. You're lucky." He grabs my hand. "Let's go. You better stand over here where it's safer." He leads me to the back of the room, his arm wrapped around my shoulder as he protects me from the crowd.

"I don't want to ruin the show for you," I protest. "You can go back. I'll wait back here."

"Are you crazy?" Ben says. "I'm not leaving you

alone." My heart thumps and the butterflies in my stomach return. A lock of hair falls over his eyes. I want to reach out and brush it back with my hand. Instead I just nod and say, "Thanks."

We spend the rest of the show standing in the back. I'm so short that it's hard to see much of the band, except an occasional blurry glimpse of the lead singer's head in between the dark mass of bodies jumping up and down in front of the dimly lit stage. Hearing the band isn't a problem—they're so loud! But I really like the music—it's so exciting.

Even though I've stopped crying and am finally having fun again, I still feel bad that Ben can't be closer to the stage. He's so kind to hang out back here with me. I peek at Ben. His head bobs up and down to the music, which means he's still having a good time.

I wish the band could play longer. The show ends sooner than I want it to. The houselights flood the club. Ben turns to me. "Sorry about your glasses," he says. "I hope you still had fun."

I'm about to say, "Yes, I did have fun," but to my horror, instead, like a really bad dream, the words that pop out of my mouth are: "Ben, I like you so much."

Oh. My. God. Please. I did not just say that. I close my eyes.

And then I open my eyes because it's stupid to close your eyes, hoping everything, especially Ben Wheeler, will disappear because, well, things simply don't disappear just because you want them to go away.

My hands tremble. It's kind of funny when you think about it—I recently performed the Mendelssohn Violin Concerto for an audience of at least five hundred people, but that doesn't come close to the dread I feel right now standing in the middle of a club in front of a silent Ben Wheeler.

"Patti." Please, don't say my name, I want to shout. I know what my name is.

Ben places a hand on my shoulder, the warmth from his palm seeping through my skin. He takes a step closer. For a moment, I wonder if he's going to kiss me, and for that brief millisecond of my life, everything takes on a brilliant sheen, all the colors around me vibrant, and I swear I can even see the color of the air. In this one moment, I see a different life for me, one where I'm a girl who's just been kissed and whose future seems filled with promise.

"Patti, I'm sorry," he says quietly. "I just like you as a friend. I thought you knew Stephanie and I were going out. I'm meeting up with her at a party later tonight after I drop you off."

And just like that, the light goes out and the world is no longer colorful but dull and washed out, like it's behind a glass shield that separates me from everyone else. I try to hide my reaction, but I can tell by the sad expression in his eyes that Ben knows exactly how I'm feeling inside.

Ben lets go of my shoulder. I blink, and finally the world disappears in a watery blur.

"I'm sorry," he says again.

I think I say something like "It's okay" or "I gotta go" or "Excuse me, I'm going to throw myself off the nearest bridge now." And that's it. That's all we have to say to each other. We walk silently out of the club and head down the street toward his car.

It's a long and quiet drive back to the church.

Correction. It is a very, very, very long and quiet drive back to the church.

As we curve around the driveway leading toward my church, I squint and notice two blurry figures standing outside the church. I can't make out their faces. I wonder who they are.

We pull up to the front of the church.

And that's when I recognize who's standing outside.

My parents.

How to Make Your Korean Parents Very Unhappy, Part I

Lie to them about attending your church's Lock-In when you're really going out with a strange boy they have never met to a see a British punk rock band in New Haven without their permission.

The Lions' Den

Samuel Kwon is weak. He's a traitor. He has no spine. Same goes for the rest of 'em.

I mean, we've read stories in youth group about missionaries who are tortured in foreign countries and still refuse to denounce God. But yet my own church youth group can't even handle a few anxious questions from my mom and dad, and betray me at the drop of a hat. I'm really glad I didn't know these guys during the days of ancient Rome. I'd be dinner for the lions by now.

Samuel claims my parents are tough interrogators. "What could we do?" he said. "We tried our best, but they knew you weren't in the bathroom for *that* long."

Eventually, bits and pieces spilled out about everything—secretly visiting Ben to jam and play music, the Lock-In deception, and sneaking out to the Blister show.

What on earth were my parents doing at Lock-In? Turns out my parents also knew the SAT scores were being posted at midnight online. They knew my password (of course) and they couldn't wait for me. So they went ahead and logged onto the website to find my scores.

The good news? I scored a 2300 on the SATs. (750 Math, 760 Verbal, 790 Writing!!!)

The bad news? My parents were so excited and proud of me that they rushed to the church to deliver the good news.

Samuel tried to distract them when they arrived at the church, but they eventually found out I was not there. Which led to the apparently grueling torture session of questions and Samuel caving in, telling them everything. "It was like the Spanish Inquisition," Samuel told me. "We were in the lions' den and everything."

"The Spanish Inquisition started in 1478 and there were no lions," I snapped back.

I slump in the backseat as my parents drive me

home, yelling the entire way. Most of it's in Korean, because when they get really mad, they sort of lose control of their English skills.

"[*Angry Korean words*] . . . how could you lie to us . . . [*angry Korean words*] . . . I'm so disappointed in you."

"We work so hard for you and . . . [*angry Korean words*] . . . this is how you repay us? . . ."

"[*Angry Korean words*] . . . we can never trust you again."

". . . and you can never see that boy again."

Eventually they stop yelling. No one talks for the rest of the ride home.

For the second time in one night, the silence is so loud.

How to Make Your Korean Parents Not So Mad at You, Part 1

Never leave the house again except to go to school and orchestra rehearsal and church.

Top Ten Ways to Avoid Ben Wheeler at School

1. Show up late to homeroom.
2. When he smiles at you in homeroom, look away.
3. Hide behind a book until the bell rings for first period.
4. Don't look him in the eye.
5. Be the first one to leave homeroom as soon as the bell rings again.
6. Turn and walk the other way if you see him heading in your direction down the hall.
7. Pretend you don't hear him when he calls out your name as you are walking away.
8. Don't look at him during gym class.
9. Hide in the library as usual during lunch hour.
10. Realize that by Thursday, Ben is avoiding you, too.

7:59 A.M. on a Friday

This has been the Longest. Week. Of. My. Life. I rush into homeroom before the first bell rings.

To my surprise and relief, Ben is not sitting at his desk. I slump back in my chair and pull out a book and pretend to read.

After a few minutes, I hear someone laugh. I can't help but look up.

It's Stephanie and Ben. They're holding hands as they enter. "I can't wait for Jet Pack tomorrow," Stephanie says as she and Ben head toward her desk. "I'm so glad you decided to come along." She sits down. Ben hovers nearby.

"You know I can't stand Jet Pack," he says. "But hey . . . I'll go for you." He smiles at her.

The bell rings. I glance at the clock—the bell's off by a minute. It's only 7:59 A.M. First period starts at eight o'clock.

Ben squeezes Stephanie's hand tightly, as if reluctant to let go. I wonder what it must be like to have someone care that much for you.

And that's when Ben leans over, closes his eyes, and kisses Stephanie tenderly on the lips.

It's 7:59 A.M. on a Friday, and I hate the fact that for the rest of my life, I will never forget this exact date and time marking the moment Ben and Stephanie kissed, and how during those few seconds everyone in the world, including me, disappeared for them.

Caesar's Last Breath

I stand by my bedroom window. There was a surprise blizzard today, burying our entire town under mounds of snow.

A cold blast of air still seeps its way through the space underneath my windowsill. The wood has warped, and I can't seal the window shut.

My dad has come up with a crude way of blocking the chill for the night by covering the windows with thick sheets of plastic. Right now, he's kneeling by the window, surrounded by several thick plastic sheets along with his toolbox and a large roll of silver duct tape.

I hold the ends of the plastic sheets to the wall

above the window frame. My dad unrolls the tape and proceeds to seal the plastic against the wall to prevent air from leaking. He then unrolls the silvery duct tape down toward the floor, sealing both of the sides and the bottom.

"There," he says. "Now you won't be cold." He pauses, as if about to crack a silly joke, like he usually does around me, but instead remains silent. I want to ask him to help me with some of my calculus homework, but I'm afraid he'll say he's too busy, and that will make me cry, so I just mumble, "Thanks."

He nods and gathers up his tools and leaves without saying another word.

Ever since the Blister/Lock-In Incident, things have been very quiet in the house. Every now and then my parents will ask about my grades, but the constant nagging and pressure have subsided. I almost miss it.

Heavy plastic covers the window. I stare through it—the world outside is hazy and blurry.

It's almost eight o'clock. Right now Stephanie and Ben are at the Fox Theatre, and Jet Pack is probably walking onstage at this very moment.

In AP physics, we learned about something known

as Caesar's Last Breath. Basically, legend has it that every breath you take contains molecules from the last breath exhaled by Julius Caesar. According to my physics teacher, if Julius Caesar's last breath were one liter of air, it would be made up of 10,000,000,000,-000,000,000,000 molecules. Atoms never disappear, so scientists theorize those very same molecules have been mixed into the entire Earth's atmosphere, a total of 5.1×10^{18} kilograms of air, or 10^{44} molecules (that's 100,000,000,000,000,000,000,000,000,000,000,000,-000,000,000 molecules). Which means every time you breathe, you're probably inhaling at least one molecule of Julius Caesar's last breath.

Right now, Stephanie and Simon Taylor from Jet Pack are breathing the very same air. I haven't spoken to Ben since the Lock-In Incident. On Monday I'll be back in school, sitting in homeroom and breathing the same air with Ben but not speaking at all.

Life can't get any worse than this.

Top Ten Awkward Moments With Ben at School

1. You make eye contact with Ben Monday morning during homeroom. He nods and says, "Hi." You nod and say "Hi" back. End of conversation.
2. Before AP English your notebook gets wedged in your locker door. Ben helps you pull it out. You say "Thank you." He says "You're welcome." You then head off in opposite directions.
3. You accidentally make eye contact with Ben Tuesday morning during homeroom. You look away before he can say anything.
4. You're heading down the hallway when you see Stephanie and Ben kiss by his locker. You keep walking.
5. You accidentally make eye contact with Ben again during homeroom. He says "Hi." You just nod and sit down, silent.
6. During gym class you accidentally kick the

soccer ball out of bounds. Ben kicks it toward you.

7. You accidentally make eye contact with Ben *again* during homeroom.

8. They're selling Senior Prom tickets at the school entrance. Ben is waiting in line. He says "Hi" as you pass by. You say "Hi" back and keep walking.

9. You're on your way to AP physics. You pass by Ben's Latin II class. You accidentally make eye contact with him. You both look away.

10. You successfully avoid making eye contact with Ben Friday morning during homeroom. You are very relieved there are only six hours left until the weekend.

My Mom's Spam Recipe #3—
Spam Kimbap (Aka Spam Sushi Rolls)

Ingredients:

1 can of Spam
1 jar of kimchi
2 cups washed and cooked white sticky rice[11]
Rice wine vinegar
Sugar
Salt
Shoyu (or just any soy sauce)
Mirin (Japanese sweet rice wine)
1 cucumber
1 carrot
Spinach
Nori (seaweed sushi wrappers)

Directions:

1. In a separate pan, boil equal parts rice wine
   vinegar and sugar (I usually use ½ cup each) plus

[11]By now I'm assuming you purchased a rice cooker or you know how
to cook rice in a pot of water.

a teaspoon of salt. Boil until the sugar dissolves.

2. Once the rice has cooked and cooled, mix as much of the vinegar sauce as you want with the rice. (But go easy on this vinegar stuff—it's really sweet.)

3. In another pan, boil equal parts shoyu (or any type of soy sauce) with sugar and mirin (I usually use ¼ cup each).

4. Once the sugar dissolves, lower the heat and then plunk down a couple slices of Spam in it and let it simmer for a few minutes.

5. Then take the Spam out and cut them into French fry–style slices.

6. Julienne some carrots and cucumbers, cook up some frozen spinach and drain it, and set aside.

7. Spread a thin layer of rice on top of one sheet of nori. Layer a row of Spam with the carrots, spinach, and cucumber in the middle of the nori sheet.

8. Carefully roll the nori into a sushi roll. This can get really messy, especially if you try to pile too much rice and Spam together (the seaweed is very delicate and can rip). Of course, my mom

always makes perfect Spam *kimbap*, while mine always fall apart and I have to spoon the mess into a bowl and just eat it with a fork.

9. Anyway, once you've rolled the Spam sushi, cut into 1-inch pieces and eat with a bunch of kimchi on the side.

10. Enjoy!

Someone knocks on my door. "Come in," I say, not getting up from my desk.

My mom enters, carrying a tray. "I thought you might want a snack," she says. "You've been studying all night."

I'm surprised by this study-break snack surprise. "Thanks," I say, moving my books so she can set the tray down. "Oh, cool! *Kimbap!*" *Kimbap* is the Korean version of sushi, but instead of raw fish, we use cooked meat, egg, vegetables, and rice wrapped in dried seaweed.

I pop one into my mouth. Oh great. Spam. It's my mom's special Spam *kimbap*. Even though I'm sick of Spam, I force a smile. "This is really good."

My mom pulls up a chair and sits beside me. "What are you working on?"

I hold up two books—Tennessee Williams's *The*

Glass Menagerie and Arthur Miller's *Death of a Salesman*. "Essay for AP English due Monday. I have to compare these two plays."

"What do these plays have in common?"

I'm surprised—my mom never asks me *about* my homework. She only asks if I've *finished* my homework. "Dreams. Both plays deal with characters who have dreams that are never realized."

"Broken dreams," she says.

"Yeah."

"Like the glass unicorn that breaks."

What? How does my mom know about that scene in *The Glass Menagerie*? Before I can ask, my mom suddenly says, "I felt so bad for Laura—her favorite glass animal was no longer unique when the horn broke off."

I'm stunned. My mom continues. "I had trouble understanding *Death of a Salesman* when I first read it, because some of the expressions were odd, like 'dime a dozen.'"

"That means you're just average. You're nothing special."

She nods. "That's what the son thought of his father."

"I didn't know you read these plays."

"I read them in high school. I read the Korean translations first, and then when I learned English, I reread them. I wanted to study literature in college and become a writer. I read so many books that I got headaches."

This is the most my mom has ever said to me about her life in Korea. "I didn't know that," I say.

"But I realized that was a silly dream," she says. "There's no guarantee that you can make a living as a writer. It's very difficult to get published. Your father had just gotten his first job in America, and I had to study something more practical. I never dreamed I would end up being a pharmacist." A shadow flickers across her eyes. She stands up. "I better leave," she says. "Good luck with your essay."

"Thanks," I say. After my mom leaves, I try to work on my essay, but I can't come up with an opening sentence. All I can think of are the words *dime a dozen*, and I wonder if that's what drives my mom and dad, if the last thing they want for themselves— or me—is to be anything ordinary.

How to Lie One More Time to Your Hard-Working and Honest Korean Parents Because You Feel You Have No Other Choice, Part I

When you receive a letter from the Juilliard admissions office congratulating you on your "most impressive" application and "beautiful" prescreening audition tape and inviting you to the campus for a live audition, you . . .

a) Hide the letter from your parents.
b) Call the Juilliard admissions office to confirm that yes, you will definitely show up on Saturday, March 21, at 2 P.M. for your live audition.
c) Call Samuel Kwon for backup.
d) All of the above.

How to Lie One More Time to Your Hard-Working and Honest Korean Parents Because You Feel You Have No Other Choice, Part 2

It's the most sublime sound I have ever heard in my life. It's the opening melody of the Mendelssohn Violin Concerto. It's plaintive, lyrical, and exquisite.

Too bad it's not me playing. I lower my violin from my shoulder and strain to hear better. "Maybe this wasn't such a good idea."

"You'll be fine." Samuel doesn't look up as he says this. He's too busy taking a practice AP calculus test.

It's ten minutes before my audition. Samuel and I are waiting in one of the designated practice rooms on

267

the second floor of the Juilliard School. It's just a plain classroom filled with desks, a dry-erase board, and a lecture podium. My violin case sits on the teacher's desk. I warmed up with some scales and arpeggios before running through the Bach and Paganini—no mistakes! But now I'm distracted because of that student across the hall playing the Mendelssohn. He or she sounds *amazing*—not good for my nerves.

"Stop listening to her," Samuel says. "Or him. Besides, they're rushing the sixteenth notes. Can't you hear it?"

I open the door and listen. After a couple moments I shut the door. "You're right," I say, no longer feeling nervous.

"See?" Samuel goes back to his book.

I smile. I have to give Samuel credit. He did a good job in arranging this trip. Our cover story? We convinced our parents that after today's orchestra rehearsal, we would be meeting our church youth group for an AP calculus practice test session and dinner.

Technically this is not a lie. We *are* meeting Tiffany and the others in West Hartford for an AP calculus study session . . . the only tiny lie is that we'll be meeting them *after* my audition.

It's pretty impressive, the spreadsheet schedule Samuel programmed the night before. So far, we're right on time:

9 A.M.	Samuel picks Patti up for her 10 A.M. violin lesson. Drive to New Haven train station.
10:32 A.M.	Samuel and Patti take 10:32 A.M. Metro North train from New Haven to New York.
12:12 P.M.	Samuel and Patti arrive at Grand Central. Grab fast food for lunch. Take the subway to Lincoln Center.
1 P.M.	Arrive at Lincoln Center. Check into Juilliard School and get assigned to a practice room.
1:15 P.M.	Warm up before audition.
2 P.M.	Audition.
4:07 P.M.	Take Metro North train from Grand Central back to New Haven.
6:56 P.M.	Arrive in New Haven. Drive to West Hartford to meet church youth group for dinner.
10:00 P.M.	Arrive home. Parents have no idea you've been in New York all day.

The person practicing in the other room has just started playing the octaves at the end of page one. I hold my breath—the octaves are a little sloppy.

"Stop comparing yourself to them," Samuel says.

"I'm not—"

"Patti, I can read your mind right now. You've got that look."

"What look?"

"You know, the look." Samuel squints. "That look. You're always listening to other violinists in rehearsal, waiting for them to trip up. And then when they make a mistake, you do this." He relaxes his eyes and smiles.

"I'm not smiling," I say.

"It's in your eyes." He returns to his book.

My palms feel cold. I rub them together. Someone knocks on our door. A woman enters. "Patti Yoon?" she asks.

I nod.

"Come on in," she says, smiling warmly. "We're ready for you."

Samuel awkwardly pats my shoulder. "Break a leg," he says.

"Thanks," I say. "I can't believe you're here. You're

always worried about getting caught for breaking the rules."

Samuel grins. "It's because you've been a bad influence on me."

I give him a quick kiss on the cheek. He turns beet red. "Thanks for being a great friend," I say.

Then I follow the woman down the hall to the audition room. We pass other designated practice rooms, a cacophony of Mendelssohn, Bach, Bartók, Prokofiev, and Beethoven filling the air as everyone warms up for their auditions. It reminds me of All-State auditions, and that relaxes me. We enter the audition room, the doors slamming shut behind me.

Four faculty members sit at a long table in the front of the classroom. They all hold clipboards and pens, ready to jot down notes if they like what they hear . . . or if I make a mistake.

"Let's start with a four-octave major and minor scale," the woman says as she joins the others at the table. "How about in the key of E?"

I raise my violin up and play an E major and E minor scale. My tone is rich, my bow arm strong, and I play every single note perfectly in tune. As soon as I finish, the woman raises her hand. "Patti, I meant a relative minor scale."

My stomach shrinks. I can't believe I've already made such a huge mistake. My fingers tremble as I quickly run through a C sharp minor scale. Fortunately I play this scale in tune too.

"Let's hear some of the Paganini, please," the woman says.

I barely get through the first few lines when she raises her hand. I stop playing. "Thank you, that'll be all. We'd like to hear the Bach."

I get through half a page of the Bach when she raises her hand again. Why does she keep stopping me? Do I sound that bad? I haven't made any mistakes. "Thank you," she says.

Meanwhile the other faculty members don't even look up at me. Their heads are bent over, their shoulders hunched, as they scribble furiously away on their clipboards. These guys mean business. This is *Juilliard*, the best music school in the country . . . in fact, probably the world. It's so surreal that I'm even here.

"We'd like to hear the Mendelssohn," the woman says.

I nod and raise the violin back to my shoulder. I close my eyes, and I tell myself to relax. All I have to do is play the Mendelssohn without a single mistake.

I shut out the judges and the blinking fluorescent lights. I pretend I'm back onstage with my youth orchestra, performing for a huge audience. The classroom disappears, the judges and their clipboards disappear, and I'm now in my own world. As I play, I suddenly remember seeing Ben in the audience with the red light flashing from his digital recorder. Somehow the image comforts me. I think about how happy he made me feel, how happy I felt when we rehearsed together, and how much fun we had in homeroom together.

This translates into the music, and I'm no longer nervous. I'm having fun playing for the judges. When I finish, the woman with the clipboard smiles. And when she shakes my hand and says I did a great job, I know in my heart she's telling the truth.

It is the shortest train ride back to Connecticut. I can't stop smiling the entire way home.

Busted

I'm finishing my econ homework in the library during lunch when someone taps my shoulder. I freeze, wondering if it's Ben.

It's not. It's Susan. "Did you hear?" she asks.

"Haven't gotten any college letters yet," I say. "We still have a couple weeks before they send them out."

She shakes her head. "I'm talking about Eric." I have never seen Susan look so happy before.

"What are you talking about?"

She grins. "He got busted! He got caught ditching school to go home and check the mail!" She snorts. "They mailed out the UConn acceptance letters this

274

week. He didn't want his parents to find out first, in case he was rejected."

"What happened to him?"

Susan shrugs. "I don't know if he got a letter or not, but he got suspended for the rest of the week!"

"Oh my God!" I shout. "That's so funny!" We crack up. I want to dance on top of my study carrel, I am so happy. "What goes around comes around," I say.

"That's not all," Susan says. "Everyone's talking about it. Because he's skipped school so much this year, he won't be able to walk across the stage for graduation."

I stop laughing. Susan stares at me. "Don't tell me you feel sorry for him," she says. "Come on, he's such a jerk."

"I know, but . . ." I pause. "What about his mom and dad? What if they already invited other family members and friends to the ceremony? That is so humiliating."

"He deserves it," Susan says. "I'm not going to feel sorry for him."

"I don't feel sorry for him," I say. "I feel sorry for his parents." Who knew Eric, with his so-called good looks and popularity, was just as stressed as the rest of us about college? I thought he had it all. Turns out he didn't.

Good Enough

"Mom, it's perfect!" Stephanie squeals. She bursts from the fitting room, clad from head to toe in a bright-red strapless form-fitting slim gown. She looks like a glamorous actress about to accept an Academy Award.

I'm standing just a few feet away in front of another nearby full-length mirror. I'm wearing a long black skirt and a plain white blouse. I look like a restaurant hostess about to seat a family of four. I can't believe Stephanie would shop here at Target. I thought she frequented the more high-end, trendy dress boutiques.

Stephanie's mother walks over and looks at the price tag on the dress. "At least it's on sale," she says, sighing.

"Mom!" Stephanie rolls her eyes. "It's not that expensive." She looks at her reflection again. "If only Ben could see me now." She twirls around, giggling. She loses her balance and bumps into me.

"Oh. Patti." She finally notices me. "What are you doing here?" Her voice has taken on that very formal "I'm pretending to be polite to you because our parents are nearby" tone. "Is that for the prom?"

"It's my All-State orchestra uniform."

"All-State? Really?" Is it me, or does she sound impressed?

"Yeah," I say. "I'm assistant concertmaster." Her eyes widen. Even though I'm sure Stephanie has no idea what "assistant concertmaster" means, I can tell she is *definitely* impressed.

"Wow," she says.

It's kind of weird—Stephanie and I are having a nice moment together. I wonder if this will disrupt the time-space continuum, like that *Star Trek* episode when . . .

277

"Stephanie," her mother calls, "I don't have all day."

"Mom, I know, I'll go change." Stephanie heads for the fitting room.

I glance at my reflection once more. Since the "body wave perm" disaster, my hair has finally settled into this curvy 1940s pageboy style. My new glasses with their thick black frames actually look retro cool. Maybe I'll borrow Tiffany's lipstick next time I see her.

I untuck the white blouse. The blouse is tapered and falls just below my waistline. It creates a nice hourglass figure, and I no longer look like I work at a restaurant. Not bad, Patti! For once, I don't think I'm that plain. It's a nice feeling.

I go back to the fitting room and change back to my shirt and jeans. Afterward I find my dad, and we stand in line at the cash register. Stephanie and her mom soon join us. We stand there, silent. After a few minutes, my dad steps out of line. "I'll be right back," he says. "Stay here."

"Where are you going?"

"I saw some socks on sale," he says. "I'll be back in a second."

My dad is still gone when it's now our turn at the register. I place the skirt and blouse on the counter. The cashier starts to add up the prices. What's taking my dad so long?

The cashier rings up the price, with my dad still lost. The cashier rings up the subtotal and looks at me expectantly. I don't have enough cash, and I don't have a credit card. I glance around—where is my dad?

"This is ridiculous," Stephanie's mom says, hissing. Her icy blue eyes narrow. "Where did that Chinese man go?"

My ears prick up at the words *Chinese man*. What does my dad's ethnicity have to do with this? He's not even Chinese. If he were white, would Mrs. Thomas have said, "Where did that man go?"

"Mom . . ." Stephanie says.

My dad finally returns. I glance at the clock on the wall—even though it seemed like an eternity, he was actually gone only for a couple minutes. A little on the inconvenient side, but it's not that big a deal. "Sorry," he says. "I wanted to get some socks that were on sale in the men's department, but I got lost." He hands the cashier his credit card.

The cashier, confused, forgets the subtotal and tries to start a new sale. The register jams.

"I need to find my manager," the cashier says. "I'll be right back." She heads off.

"This is enough." Mrs. Thomas raises her voice.

My dad turns around. "I'm sorry," he says, smiling politely.

But Mrs. Thomas doesn't care. "There are people waiting," she snaps. "That was so rude of you to just take off like that."

I feel dizzy.

"Mom . . ." Stephanie says, tugging at her mother's elbow.

The cashier and her manager return. "Ma'am, is there a problem?" he asks Mrs. Thomas first.

"Yes," she says. "He held up the line. Don't these people understand how it works? You stay in line, you don't just leave!"

"Ma'am, please be patient. I have to put the key in the register to cancel the sale. She'll ring up the sale again and then you'll have your turn. I apologize for the inconvenience."

The manager turns the key to the register and cancels the order.

"Dad, forget it," I say. "I can wear last year's All-State uniform."

My dad faces Stephanie's mom again. "I'm sorry," he says politely. "It was my mistake."

"What?" Stephanie's mom looks puzzled.

"My mistake."

She nudges Stephanie. "Is he speaking English?"

Of course he's speaking English, I want to tell Stephanie's mom. But for the first time, I hear my dad the way other people might—with a heavy Korean accent. I'm used to the way my parents speak—I'm so used to it that I forget that they have heavy accents. Maybe it's difficult for Stephanie's mom to understand my dad.

Wait a minute—why am I trying to find an excuse for Mrs. Thomas? It's not difficult for the store manager to understand my dad's accent. In fact, everyone else has always understood my dad's English. Why is Stephanie's mom being so rude?

"I'm sorry," my dad says one last time before turning around to face the cashier.

"Unbelievable," Mrs. Thomas says loudly. She towers over me, her fair skin pulled taut against her cheekbones

281

as she grimaces at us. She shares Stephanie's bright blond hair and high cheekbones, but there's a brittle quality to her beauty, as if she might snap in two if you touched her. She rolls her eyes at Stephanie. She lowers her voice as she speaks to her daughter, but I can hear every word. "These people, they come to our country, they don't bother learning the language. . . ."

These people. I realize there's nothing I can say or do that will calm Mrs. Thomas down. I glance at Stephanie, and there's this stricken look on her face, as if she's just been slapped, all the blood draining away from her cheeks. She opens her mouth as if to say something, then stops and looks away.

I'm forced to wait as the cashier does our sale all over again. My dad has to sign his initials on the original receipt, which causes Mrs. Thomas to sigh very loudly and tap her foot. "These people . . ." she says again.

"Mom, they're standing right there," Stephanie whispers.

"They don't understand . . ."

"Mom, Patti speaks English."

Mrs. Thomas finally shuts up.

Finally the sale is complete. The cashier hands me

the plastic shopping bag with my skirt and shirt. We leave without saying thank you.

I'm numb as we head down the escalator toward the parking garage. My dad doesn't say a word.

We get into the car. As we head home, my dad turns the radio on to the classical music station. "Hey, it's the Mendelssohn!" he says, just a little too enthusiastically. "Who's playing this?"

"Sarah Chang," I say.

"She's very good," my dad says, still smiling. I notice the deep lines around the corners of his eyes and the way his lips twitch as he struggles to keep smiling all the way home. My dad heard everything Stephanie's mom said. He looks hurt. I have never seen my dad look this upset before. I feel so helpless and frustrated, because there's nothing I can do to make him feel better.

My dad graduated from the most prestigious university in Korea and designs computer software for some of the largest banks in New England. Even though he has a thick Korean accent, he speaks fluent English. And he has a daughter—me—who has a very good shot of getting into Harvard, Yale, and Princeton.

But to people like Stephanie's mom none of that

matters, because the only thing she can—and will ever—see is the color of our skin. So what's the point of getting into a good college and becoming successful, if in the end I'll still run into more people like Stephanie's mom who will never, ever believe that I'm good enough?

SORRY

I tie my wet hair back into a ponytail and shove my dirt-stained sneakers into the locker. Gym wasn't too awful today. We're doing softball, and for once, I hit the ball! I actually made it to first base without getting tagged out. The bell rang before we could complete the game, and I was almost a little disappointed.

I've got two minutes left before AP English. I turn to leave and bump into Stephanie.

"Patti," she says, "I was looking for you."

I think about what happened Saturday at the store. I've replayed that scene a hundred times in my head, how her mother insulted my dad, and I realize: I don't have to talk to this girl at all. So I ignore her. I walk past her and head out of the locker room. I hear her footsteps behind me.

"Patti," she says.

I don't stop walking. But it feels a little weird to be acting so rudely, not like me at all. I have to force myself to keep going down the hall.

She rushes after me. "Patti, please—I have to say something."

I finally stop. "Yes?" I say, polite but not friendly.

"My mom . . . she didn't mean what she said." Stephanie takes a deep breath. "I'm really sorry, Patti."

Stephanie is apologizing to me? I'm floored. I have no idea what to say.

I look at her closely. She didn't reapply her makeup after gym class. I have never seen her without her makeup on. Her lips are much thinner without all that lipstick and gloss, and her left eye is slightly higher than her right, like an early Picasso painting. Her skin is pale and washed out, with a spray of freckles across her nose that I've never noticed before. She looks tired under the fluorescent lights.

"What is it?" she asks.

"Nothing," I say.

She nods. "Yeah, it wasn't that big a deal."

"No," I say. "When I said 'nothing,' I didn't mean—"

"The whole thing was so embarrassing," she says, lowering her voice as if we're sharing some kind of secret.

Embarrassing? She's talking about her mom and my dad, the things her mother said about my father, as if he couldn't understand, as if we weren't even there. If Stephanie was looking for absolution, she has totally blown it.

"It wasn't embarrassing." The words burst out of me. "It was *humiliating*. I know she's your mom, but she was *wrong*." I don't think I've ever said so many words to Stephanie before in my life. But even though I'm angry, it feels right. I couldn't just let her think her mother's attitude was no big deal.

There's a long moment of silence. Stephanie's shoulders slump. "I'm sorry I didn't say more at the store," she says.

My mind is going a thousand miles per hour, and the silence stretches again. "Whatever," I say at last, and I walk away.

I know my dad would be horrified by what I've just done. He would have wanted me to accept her apology, dismissing the whole thing quietly. He'd never understand why I couldn't keep my head down and my mouth shut. I barely understand it myself.

But if this is what rocking the boat feels like, I think I like it.

The image of my dad driving home, trying to hide how upset he was, pops into my head. How many times has that sort of thing happened to him before?

I think of his struggle to remain polite to Mrs. Thomas and of the ride afterward, listening to the Mendelssohn in silence. I see his hands tight on the steering wheel and the corners of his mouth straining to smile. And I think maybe he would understand, after all.

Church Youth Group Can Be Fun!

Kyung Hee wants the seniors in our church youth group to do something special for our annual Spring Show.

"It'll be fun," she says. "Patti plays violin, Tiffany does ballet, Samuel plays the cello. I think it would be neat if the seniors did something that showcased everyone's talents. That will show the younger students church youth group is fun!"

We come up with a lot of silly ideas, everything from a mock infomercial to an interpretive dance. Finally we decide to write a song together and perform it.

"What are we going to call ourselves?" Samuel asks.

"We should come up with a cool name for our group."

"How about the Woodward Korean United Methodist Church Youth Group Musicians?" Isaac suggests.

Dead silence fills the room.

"Okay, how about Jet Pack?" Tiffany suggests.

"They're already a band," Samuel says. Tiffany shrugs.

"How about P.K.D.?" I ask.

"Intriguing," Samuel says. "What does P.K.D. stand for?"

"Perfect Korean Daughter," I say.

There's another moment of silence, and then everyone bursts out laughing. Tiffany falls back on the couch and covers her face with a throw pillow. Isaac snorts, which makes me giggle even more. Samuel's face twitches as he tries not to smile, but he can't hold it in and finally starts laughing.

I remember when I first started going to church as a little kid, and how I've practically grown up with these guys. It will be so different in the fall, when we are in college. We won't see each other every Sunday—we'll probably see each other only during the holidays. I remember when we were six years old, how Tiffany and

I used to hide under the pews after the sermon, trying not to giggle as our parents looked for us. How Sally and I did each other's hair during our first Lock-In together in the eighth grade. I remember when Samuel was eight and accidentally sat on the birthday cake hidden in the rec room as a surprise for our pastor. Isaac and James and Lisa desperately tried to put the cake back together while Samuel bawled in the corner.

I'm really going to miss these guys next year.

And, of course, Bible Pictionary.

Don't Think, Just Play

I'm sitting onstage at the Jorgensen Center for the Performing Arts at the University of Connecticut's Storrs campus on a Saturday morning. The seats are littered with open instrument cases as people rosin their bows, tweak their reeds, and warm up.

I've got ten minutes before our morning All-State rehearsal starts. I run through some of the more difficult passages in the music.

"Hi." A scrawny kid sits down next to me.

"You can't sit there," I say. "My stand partner hasn't shown up yet."

"I am your stand partner," he says. He places his

sheet music on the stand. "Maurice Lanier. Concert-master."

This is our All-State Concertmaster? He can't be more than . . .

I recognize his name from the All-State list. But . . .

"I skipped the seventh and eighth grades," Maurice explains without me even asking. "I'm in the ninth grade, so I qualified for All-State."

Holy crap. A twelve-year-old beat me.

This is not how I pictured my first meeting with the All-State concertmaster. It's too abrupt. I had daydreamed about practicing the music at our stand and the concertmaster standing just a few feet away, mesmerized by my tone and virtuosity. "I can't believe I'm sitting ahead of someone as brilliant as you," he would then say.

Turns out Maurice sneaked up on me and was listening to me practice for the past five minutes. He sits down, puts his violin and bow on his lap, reaches for the pencil on the music stand, and starts erasing my fingerings.

Fingerings are the little numbers—1, 2, 3, 4—that violinists write above certain notes to remind them what position and finger they should shift to while playing.

There's a real art to fingerings—some people believe you should avoid using your left pinky at all possible times because it's your weakest finger, and you should always shift up to your third—your ring finger. Other people believe you should shift on the second finger, not the first, so you have less of a "sliding" sound as your fingers scamper up and down the fingerboard. And so on. . . . Anyway, what I'm trying to say is that I spent a long time on these fingerings, and I don't appreciate Maurice rudely erasing them without asking my permission.

"Excuse me," I say, grabbing the pencil away just as he's writing "3" over my "4." (Great. He's one of those violinists who avoid using the pinky.)

He studies the rest of my penciled-in fingerings. He shakes his head.

"I think we should use my fingerings," he says. "After all, I'm concertmaster and the entire section should not only follow my bowings but also my fingerings. That way we can sound like one violin." He points to the music. "I don't know why you stay in first position and play the open A string. You should shift to third position and play the A on the D string. That way the sharp tone of the open A string won't jar the listener."

Oh. My. God. I glance at my watch. Lunch is three hours away.

It's going to be a *long* rehearsal.

I hand my pencil back to Maurice, who triumphantly erases the rest of my fingerings. I lean back in my chair, wishing I played a different instrument.

Then I spot Ben entering from stage left. He holds his trumpet in one hand, his music folder in the other. He's wearing a black jean jacket, black T-shirt, and faded jeans.

It's funny how my stomach still twists into knots when I see Ben. Even though it's been more than two months since the Lock-In Incident, my insides hurt every time I look at him. We're polite to each other in homeroom, but we no longer trade CDs or talk about music. It's just "Hi, how are you?" and that's it. I wish I had never told him how I felt. I would give anything to take that moment back. Now whenever I remember our jam sessions or conversations about music in homeroom, each memory is tainted.

But I don't have time to obsess about Ben right now, because our All-State conductor, Ms. Alice Neale, has just entered. Everyone takes their seats and waits for Ms.

Neale as she steps onto the podium. She's the conductor for the New Haven Symphony Orchestra and a member of the Yale faculty.

Ms. Neale nods at our stand. I half rise from my seat because I'm used to being concertmaster and having to tune the orchestra. But I stop when I remember I'm assistant concertmaster. I sit back down and grit my teeth as Maurice stands up and says loudly, "Winds and brass." The oboist plays a long A while the winds and brass players tune their instruments. Maurice nods again and the oboist plays another long A. Maurice raises his violin and begins tuning. That's the strings' cue to tune as well.

"Welcome to All-State," Ms. Neale says. "Let's run through the Rimsky-Korsakov first."

She raises her baton and gives the downbeat. The movement opens with a precise military snare-drum roll, followed immediately by the trumpet fanfare.

Maurice plays the first of several concertmaster solos in the suite. The ones I was supposed to play.

I close my eyes and listen, really listen. He's flawless. Not one missed note, not one fumbled rhythm. His bow doesn't scratch against the strings. He's perfect. But as

Maurice continues to play, my mind starts to wander. I glance at Ms. Neale, who looks a little bored. Maurice is technically perfect. But he plays like a machine—there's no emotion behind his playing.

Halfway through the movement, after the flute, clarinet, oboe, and harp solos, our violin section falls apart during our big moment—the main melody of the movement. Some people are holding the whole note too long while others rush and play faster than the conductor's beat.

Ms. Neale lowers her baton. Silence. "First violins," she says, tapping her music stand. "Let's start that section again." She gives the upbeat and we play. The sound is uneven—the first two stands are able to play the notes, but the other dozen players struggle to keep up.

Ms. Neale stops conducting. "I'm surprised," she says. "You're supposed to be the best in the state, and yet no one is prepared. This music is magnificent and deserves more respect from all of you."

Maurice raises his hand. "I agree," he says. "We've all had the music for several months, which was plenty of time for everyone to learn their parts."

Oh *please*. Maurice may be a musical genius, but

he's also an insufferable, brown-nosing, *sycophantic* musical genius. (I can't believe I'm still using SAT vocab words.)

Apparently Ms. Neale feels the same way, because she just sighs and ignores Maurice. Then she points to me. "You."

"Yes?" I swear I was playing in tempo. I can't believe she's singling me out. What did I do wrong? I slink back in my seat.

"You seem to be the only one who knows the correct tempo. Please play for everyone."

She raises her baton and gives me the upbeat. *Keep looking ahead at the next measure*, I tell myself as I follow her tempo.

I reach the next concertmaster solo in the piece. I look up. Ms. Neale is still waving her baton, which means I have to keep playing. I haven't practiced the concert-master solos even though my parents kept insisting I should. These solos are very difficult, especially if you're sight-reading them for the first time, as I'm about to do.

Don't think, just play, I tell myself.

Wait a minute. Why do those words sound familiar?

It's what Ben told me during our first jam session. I plunge ahead with the solo, my fingers stumbling as I play very unfamiliar notes. But instead of feeling bad every time I hit a wrong note, I act like it's no big deal. In fact, when I miss one note, I quickly improvise a harmony to make up for it. Everything I learned about improvisation with Ben saves me from falling apart right now as I play this unfamiliar passage. I stop worrying about wrong notes and start having fun. The music comes alive. My bow sweeps across the strings with a flourish.

I reach the end of the solo. Ms. Neale signals me to stop. I lower my violin. Everyone in my section, including Maurice, taps their bows against their stands.

"That was really good," Maurice whispers, and to my surprise, he sounds sincere.

"Notice how she didn't play all the correct notes but still made sure to keep within the tempo?" Ms. Neale says. "She compensated for that quite nicely. What helps is if you all follow the correct bowings." She smiles at me. "You sounded beautiful." She raises her baton. "Now, brass and winds, let me hear you at the same measure."

"What grade are you in?" Maurice whispers as we wait patiently for the brass and winds to finish playing.

"I'm a senior."

"Did you apply to Juilliard?" he asks.

I nod.

"You'll get in."

"What makes you so sure?"

"I attend their Saturday precollege program," he says. "You're better than the high school seniors who are in that program."

"Thanks," I say, surprised. "Do you like Juilliard?"

He shrugs. "It's okay. Sometimes I wish I could quit the violin."

"Are you crazy?"

"I have to practice four hours a day. I have a tutor so I don't fall behind on my regular classes. I have an audition every other week and a recital once a month." He looks tired just telling me about this.

"But don't you like to play?" I ask.

"I used to. Now music is just something I *have* to do. Sometimes I wish I could do other things. There are so many other possibilities. Like skateboarding. My parents won't let me because they're afraid I'll break my arm and I'll lose my ability to play." He frowns. "That's all they care about. My violin."

The winds and brass finish playing, so we stop talking. Ms. Neale raises her baton again. "Okay, let's have everyone from the top," she says.

Maurice and I wait for the downbeat. I glance at him, and all of a sudden this twelve-year-old kid ages about fifty years in front of me. I notice dark circles under his eyes, and as we begin to play, I notice how bored he looks, how he seems to be playing on autopilot, as if he can no longer see or hear the beauty nestled inside the notes. I think about his parents and wonder how much they pressure their son, if all they care about is his success and not his happiness. Or maybe they're like my parents— they're confused and think that success and happiness are the same thing, like you can't have one without the other.

Awkward Moment No. 11 With Ben

I have no idea where I am.

After rehearsal, Susan, Samuel, and I were supposed to head back to the cafeteria for lunch. But I stayed behind because Maurice wanted to change the fingerings . . . again.

Anyway, I'm walking by myself across campus, and to my right is the Institute of Material Science building, and I'm pretty sure that's nowhere near the UConn Student Union, where we're supposed to eat lunch. My back aches, so I shift my violin case to the other shoulder. The sea of green grass and brick buildings stretches before me, endless, and my feet hurt from all this walking. I stop and scan the horizon, wondering if I should just skip lunch and head back to the auditorium. College students walk past me, but I don't want to ask anyone for directions yet. I put down my case, wipe the sweat from my forehead, and pull the campus map from my backpack, looking for the legend.

"Patti?" I look up. To my surprise, it's Ben, lugging his trumpet case in one hand, a crumpled map in the other.

"I think it's this way," I say, pointing to the right.

"No," he says. "You'll end up at the Northwest Residence Halls. I'm officially an expert on that area."

He puts down his trumpet case and leans over my shoulder to peer at my map. I can feel his breath brush across my neck. I close my eyes for a moment and try not to cry.

"Here it is," he says, pointing at the map. He steps back and picks up his trumpet case. "If we hurry, we can make it before lunch ends."

We turn around and head up North Eagleville Road. A group of students sits on the front lawn in the shade of a giant grove of trees. As we walk by, I realize Ben and I look just like these students, right down to our heavy backpacks. Those students probably think we're music majors because of our instrument cases, I think as we pass them. What is it going to be like next year, all by myself on a college campus? I can choose my own classes, I can study when I want, and I can eat whatever I want. I can be like these students, just hanging out on the lawn on a sunny Saturday afternoon instead of being forced by my parents to study. All that freedom! I can't wait.

"What's so funny?" Ben asks.

To my embarrassment, I realize I'm grinning from ear to ear. I blush. "I'm just happy. I can't believe we'll be in college next year."

"I know—it's going by so fast," Ben agrees. "My last track meet is next week, yearbooks arrive soon, the prom's in May . . ." He pauses. I glance at him and realize he's embarrassed he brought up the prom. Hello, Awkward Moment No. 11 With Ben.

You know, I could stay quiet and just concentrate on my feet as we make a left on Hillside and pass the Jorgensen auditorium. I could pretend I didn't hear him mention the prom. I could act as if I had never told him I liked him and that he had rejected me.

But I'm tired of staying quiet and playing the rules.

Time to show Ben that I'm not going to fall apart just because he rejected me. I want us to be friends again. I take a deep breath. "I ran into Stephanie at the store last week," I say cheerfully. "I saw her try on her dress for the prom. She looked beautiful." I smile. There. That was easier than I thought it would be.

Ben's green-olive eyes narrow for a moment as he processes what I've just said. "That was really nice of you," he finally says.

We continue walking, but this time the silence isn't so awkward. After a few minutes Ben speaks up. "You know those songs we wrote? I played them on my acoustic guitar and recorded them on my computer."

"That's cool," I say, excited. "How did it sound? I'd love to hear it."

"The songs sound okay," he says. "Something's still missing."

"Like a violin?" I smile. "Or maybe you'd prefer a tuba player instead 'cause we violinists can be such drama queens."

He laughs—and it's official. The awkwardness between us has ended. It's as if nothing had ever happened, as if we'd been friends for years. He wraps his arm around my shoulders and gives me a casual half hug. "Maybe you could come over and play your violin parts? I could record you on a separate track and mix them together." He pauses. "That is, if your parents will let you come over."

I smile. "We'll see. I'll ask them."

He nods. "Cool." We continue walking.

"Hey, look." He points. "There's the Student Union."

"We should've left bread crumbs to mark our trail," I say.

Ben laughs. "We'll walk back together after lunch," he says. "If I'm gonna get lost, I might as well be lost with you."

He grabs my hand and squeezes it for a moment and smiles. His hand feels warm around mine. He lets go as we enter the Student Union together. I feel a little sad, because I still really like him more than as a friend. Maybe one day this feeling will fade away. At least we're back to being friends, which is better than nothing. No more awkward moments. Ben will never kiss me, but we share something else—music. I think that's worth more than a kiss.

How to Make Your Korean Parents Very Unhappy, Part 2

I stand on my tiptoes, trying to peer over the sea of people much taller than me. Where are my parents?

I'm standing in the middle of the auditorium lobby. Our concert starts soon. I tug at the tag in the collar of my white blouse, wishing I had cut it off before getting dressed for the concert. Now it's going to itch all night and bother me. I yank at the label, but nothing happens.

My cell phone rings. I answer. "Hello?"

"Where are you?" It's Samuel. He sounds urgent.

"In the lobby. Samuel, why are you—"

307

"Act normal. I'm right outside with my parents."

"Do you know where my mom and dad are?"

"They're heading . . ." He lowers his voice. *"They're at the front entrance. Patti, get out. I repeat, get out of the lobby. Whatever you do, don't let them . . ."*

"Patti!" My mom and dad march across the lobby.

". . . see you."

I hang up the phone. "Hi," I say. "The concert starts . . ."

Oh boy. My mom is clutching several envelopes. But they're not just envelopes. They're large manila-size envelopes. Thick envelopes. With what look like college insignias in the return-address corner.

The college acceptance letters must have arrived while we were at All-State. Everything seems to move in slow motion as my mom silently hands over the pile of envelopes.

I start ripping through each envelope. *"Dear Ms. Yoon: It is our pleasure to welcome you to Yale University's Class of . . ." "Dear Ms. Yoon: Congratulations on your acceptance to Dartmouth . . ." "Dear Ms. Yoon: It is with great pleasure that the admissions committee at Cornell . . ." "Dear Ms. Yoon: Congratulations on your acceptance into*

Princeton . . ." "Dear Ms. Yoon: On behalf of the admissions committee at Columbia, we are proud to . . ." "Dear Ms. Yoon: The University of Pennsylvania would like to extend congratulations . . ."

I'm dizzy. It's over. It's finally over. I did it. Now everyone can leave me alone because I did what they wanted, I got into all the Ivy Leagues (okay, so I was wait-listed at Harvard, but Samuel was wait-listed at Yale, so I figure it all evens out in the end) . . .

. . . wait. There's still one more envelope. It's a thick packet with the words *Juilliard School of Music* stamped in the left-hand corner. I can't breathe.

I notice it's already been opened. I pull out the letter. *"Dear Ms. Yoon: Congratulations . . ."*

"I got into Juilliard," I say.

Silence. I look up. My parents aren't smiling. Hang on. I thought that they would be happy. That they would be proud. After all, I got in almost everywhere.

"You never told us you applied," my dad says.

"How could you lie to us?" my mom says.

I look at my feet. This is supposed to be the happiest moment of my life because I just got accepted into a whole bunch of Ivy Leagues, and instead it's turning out to be even worse than when Ben told me he only liked me as a friend.

I can't take this anymore. I have to say something . . . because my parents aren't the only ones here who are unhappy right now.

How to Stop Making Your Korean Parents Happy and Start Making Yourself Happy, Part 1

"Stop giving me such a hard time," I say.

There's a rushing sound in my ears as people push past me, the lights dimming to indicate that our concert is about to begin. I have only a few minutes before I have to leave to go onstage with the other musicians. The batch of envelopes in my hands feels heavy, weighing me down.

"Patti, we just give you a hard time because we want you to be successful," my dad says.

"I *am* successful," I say, my voice louder than I intended. "You raised me to be a good person and you

311

taught me to work hard. I will work hard next year in college. You don't have to worry."

"We'll always worry about you," my mom says. "That's our job. We're your parents. We know you're talented in music. That's what set you apart from the others. That's how you got into the Ivy League. But you need to be realistic about the future."

"We told you there's no security in music," my dad says. "It's not safe."

"Stop it!" I shout. My mom gasps. I've never raised my voice at my parents. Some people glance in our direction as they pass by. "Safe from what, Dad? Nothing's safe! Remember how Stephanie's mom yelled at you? She didn't care what college you went to! It's not about where you go to school or what job you have!"

"What's it about then?" my dad asks.

"It's about . . ." I hesitate. What is it about? Is it about this violin I'm holding in my hands? Is it about Ben, who's walking by with his mother and looking in my direction, an expression of concern on his face because he has obviously overheard me yelling at my parents? My vision blurs, but suddenly I can see the answer so clearly.

"It's about being happy," I say.

"You can't be happy all the time," my dad says. "It's not realistic."

"I know," I say. "But at least I'm happy when I play my violin. I'm happy when I'm hanging out with Ben. I'm happy with, oh my God, I can't believe I'm saying this, but I'm actually happy when I hang out with Samuel and my church youth group. I love when I read something like *The Glass Menagerie* in AP English and cry because the language is so beautiful and the story is so sad. Dad, I like it when you help me with my math homework, even when you get annoyed at me, because it's the only time we're together. Mom, I'm sick of Spam and never want to eat it again, but it makes me laugh when you surprise me with your late-night study snacks. I know you can't be happy all the time, but at least I know what does make me happy. And that's a start."

I don't even know what I'm saying, because I can no longer see my parents. I touch my face and it's wet. The lights flicker once more and I can vaguely hear someone announcing in the lobby that the concert will start in five minutes. I throw the envelopes onto the floor. I don't care if that was a baby thing to do. I take a deep breath and shudder because I'm crying so hard.

"Patti," my mom says, her voice choking.

But I don't answer. I turn around and walk away and leave my parents alone.

Happy

The concert goes by too quickly for me. Before I know it, we're near the last page of the Dvořák. I lean over and flip to the next page of our music. As I sit back and count the measures of rests, waiting for our turn to play again, I look at the audience. The stage lights are so bright that I can't see anything or anyone—it's all darkness. I wonder where my parents are, if they're even here or if they're still standing out in the lobby by themselves.

I glance at Maurice, whose eyes are blank as he plays. Even though his playing is flawless, I remember him telling me about how music was now something he "had" to do. If I choose Juilliard, will I become just like Maurice? I don't want music to become this thing I *have* to do, because then it won't be special anymore.

I take a deep breath as we near the end, the scent of rosin dust and the varnished maple wood of my violin comforting me. The sounds around me—a man coughing in the back row, the crackling of a candy wrapper, the squirming of some of the younger children in the front rows—all these sounds disappear.

After a few moments, all I can hear is the voice coming from my violin. It makes me truly happy. But it's not the only thing that makes me happy. Maurice was right—there are so many other things in life, so many other possibilities to make me happy. And I shouldn't have to settle for just one.

Curtain Call

Everyone crowds around backstage after the concert, lining up to deposit their music folders in the boxes by the exit door before going to the green room to put away their instruments.

I drop off my music folder and am about to head out the door when I hear my name. I look up.

It's my parents. They slowly make their way through the throng to reach me.

"It was a nice concert," my mom finally says.

"I liked the Dvořák," my dad says.

"Thanks," I mumble.

There's a long moment of silence. Then my mom

reaches over and tucks the label of my blouse back in.

"So . . . you looked happy onstage," my dad says.

I nod. More silence. My dad tries again. "What school will you choose?"

"I get to choose?" I ask.

"Of course you do," my mom says, surprised. "Have you made up your mind?"

I shake my head. "I don't know yet," I say.

"You don't want to go to Juilliard?" my dad asks. "But music makes you happy."

"It does, but I don't know if I want to go to Juilliard. I have to think about it. I want to go where I'll have a lot to choose from."

"But no matter where you go, there's no guarantee that you'll be happy," my dad says.

"I know," I say. "But at least I get to choose. That makes me happy." I think about Maurice and the dark circles under his eyes. "Mom, Dad, success and happiness, they're not the same thing."

My parents glance at each other. I can tell that they're still worried, but at least they're beginning to understand. It's a start.

"Well, I should go put away my . . ." I realize I'm

holding only my violin. "I left my bow on the stand. I better get it."

"We'll wait for you in the lobby," my mom says.

"Okay," I say.

"Hey, let's go out for ice cream," my dad says. "To celebrate!"

"What for?" I ask.

My dad holds up the envelopes. "We're very proud of you," he says.

"Thanks." My vision blurs again for a moment. When I blink, they're gone.

I walk back onto the stage. The audience has left, and the auditorium is empty. Someone has left the spotlight on, the light spilling across the conductor's podium. I feel a little sad, standing here on the empty stage. I've done All-State four years in a row, and I can't believe I won't be here next year.

I'm picking up my bow from my music stand when I hear footsteps. I turn around. It's Ben.

"Hey," he says. "I was wondering where you were."

"Forgot this." I hold up my bow.

He nods. "Hey, you looked upset in the lobby. I was worried. Is everything okay with you and your parents?"

"We're fine." My voice trembles a bit because I'm about to cry. Not because I'm sad again, but because I'm happy that Ben cares enough about me to ask.

"That's good." A lock of hair spills over his green-olive eyes. I reach up and gently sweep it to the side.

"Thanks," he says, smiling.

In a few minutes I will walk offstage and meet my parents in the lobby. They will take me out for ice cream and I will order mint chocolate chip, my favorite.

Susan and I will graduate co-valedictorians, and she will win a full scholarship to Smith College. I will finally make a decision and choose Yale because it offers me the most choices. I will apply to the special music program for incoming freshmen that Ms. Bright, my Yale alumni interviewer, told me about. I will be accepted into that program, and later I will major in English, but I will become principal second of the Yale Symphony Orchestra and I will give a recital every year in the spring, where my parents will sit in the front row, beaming and no longer afraid that I will make a mistake. During our freshman year, Samuel will sneak over to the Yale side during our first Harvard-Yale football game, and we will have a lot of fun. That's also when I will meet a cute guy named Kyle sitting near us in the stands, and he will ask me out on my first date and I will say yes.

Stephanie will go to UConn on a track scholarship. Ben will major in political science at Boston University. Ben and Stephanie will break up one week after graduation, but they will promise to remain friends forever, even though they both start dating other people and just gradually lose touch as new people and new friends fill their lives.

The last time I see Ben will be when we bump into each other in the aisle between two bookshelves in the back of the library on the last day of school. He will ask how I did on my final exams, and I will say that I'm pretty sure I aced them all. He will smile and say *Good for you*. Then the bell will ring, and we will say goodbye. I do not realize it then, but that will be the last time we will ever talk with each other, because after our graduation ceremony, my parents will whisk me away to a restaurant for lunch with Samuel and his family before I can find Ben to say good luck and good-bye.

But right now I'm still standing here on an empty

stage with Ben. We're both silent, not sure what else there is to say. And then Ben smiles at me, that familiar, wry half smile, and he puts his hand on my shoulder and is about to say something, maybe something like "I'm glad things are all right with your family," but instead he leans over and kisses me on the cheek. It's a soft, gentle kiss, really more like a platonic kiss between two friends, or a kiss between a brother and sister. It's not romantic at all.

But that's all right. Because at this very moment, as I gaze into his beautiful green-olive eyes, I realize I don't want to kiss him back. I smile as Ben lets go of me and says, "See you later," and walks offstage.

The funny thing is that I don't feel sad. My heart no longer aches. Instead my heart feels really full, and I know it will never be empty again.

I take a deep breath and gaze past the bright stage spotlight hovering above me, and I think about what will happen to me next, and I realize the possibilities are endless.

About Paula Yoo

Okay, I admit it. Like Patti Yoon, I play the violin. Yes, I was concertmaster of my Connecticut All-State High School Orchestra. And I snuck out occasionally to see a couple of cool bands (sorry, Mom & Dad). But this novel is a work of FICTION. Although I too was forced to undergo a really bad home perm, it burned my LEFT ear, not my right. And there was a cute guy in my homeroom who played rock guitar and asked me to work on a few songs with him, but his name was NOT Ben Wheeler.

When I'm not writing novels that allegedly have nothing to do with my personal life, I also write TV scripts. I was born in Virginia and grew up in Connecticut. I've also lived in Seoul, Korea; New York; Seattle; and Detroit. I now live in Los Angeles with my husband, who plays guitar—and yes, we jam occasionally, just like Patti and Ben.